EVALORE and her psychiatrist . . .

"Is your wife very beautiful?" I asked him.

"She was very beautiful."

Ah—did you hear that? —was, WAS! That's all I need to know, no, not all, I can go further, after all, I must have some fun being a patient, I can say what I like, I am *only* a patient. . . .

"Do you make love to her every night?"

He suddenly seems to wake up. Smiles. "You little devil," he says, "you certainly know where to strike." If he had said that I'm the most beautiful girl in the world it wouldn't have pleased me half as much. You little devil, he said. That makes me very happy. That's personal. That's very intimate. I'll dream about that before going to sleep. I'll grow two horns just to please him.

I'd love to please him. . . .

evalore

by

EVA JONES

FAWCETT CREST • NEW YORK

EVALORE

THIS BOOK CONTAINS THE COMPLETE TEXT
OF THE ORIGINAL HARDCOVER EDITION.

Published by Fawcett Crest Books, a unit of CBS Publications,
the Consumer Publishing Division of CBS Inc.,
by arrangement with J. B. Lippincott Company.

ISBN: 0-449-23912-8

This book is pure fiction and does not refer to any person,
living or dead. The description of the work in the hospital
is no reflection on any existing institutions which are doing
admirable work under difficult circumstances.

First published in 1976 under title: *Thirteen*

Printed in the United States of America

10 9 8 7 6 5 4 3 2 1

I love I₁lo

The soul does not age
MARGOT VON SYDOW

one

WHY doesn't she give up? God, I hate her. Amongst her bottles, creams and brushes, slapping it on. For whom, may I ask? For whom? Aha, he will be home in half an hour. He knows what she looks like, why bother? There she sits, calmly smiling into her mirror as if butter, etc. etc. A cup of her foul smelling dandelion coffee next to her. And the radio on, I just asked her a question—she didn't even hear. I think she doesn't care about me at all. All she wants is to scribble away or paint her eyelids. It's revolting, at her age. It makes me sick to think that she and . . . well, I won't think then.

Why doesn't she eat like everybody else? She's ill—she *says*. Gets up all bright-eyed in the morning and whistles. She's still whistling as she slaps more cream on at night. An athlete, a long distance runner, that's her. Ill! She just doesn't want to put on weight round the middle. She nibbles at some beatly tasteless salad leaves, gives an orange a

squeeze and that's her lunch. How she can possibly
exist on that, I wouldn't know. Bet she goes to
some quack when nobody is looking. She's sly, that
woman is. Looks at you with her small glittering
eyes and thinks nobody knows. But I know. I know
her inside out. She fools them all though. "What a
nice mother you have, she's so kind . . ." *Kind*!
She'd stick a knife into you if it suits her. Oh why
do I get upset every time she sits down at her
dressing table?

There's Illo now. I can hear the front door go.
Husband, father, what ridiculous words. His name
is Illo, Illo. People should not have labels. He's my
father. This, ladies and gentlemen, this is my
mother's husband who makes her housebound. I
wonder what she does when I'm at school. If only
she were housebound. The whole day to herself.
I've seen her looking at the Hoover, shaking short
brown curls—brown ugh! It's tinted if you please,
dyed, dyed, she's had it dyed. What did I say? She
looked at that Hoover, too much trouble she decided and went out saying: "I'll be back in a couple
of hours, Evalore." Where is she going, I wonder,
and why can't she tell me? I've got to tell *her* where
I am going. Illo never asks me. He understands me,
he knows me. He would never ask a thirteen year
old girl where she's going.

Still, he gave his consent. She made him, of
course. He would never have sent me to this absurd, ghastly clinic three times a week. That was

her idea. It's obvious—she wants me out of the way, to have him all to herself. Mondays, Wednesdays and Fridays after school. It's one of those modern OPEN CLINICS. Open! I can't breathe here it's so disgusting. What a place . . . The Patients—just look at them. I don't belong here, I'm not sick. I'm not standing in a corner with my you-know-what open, making love to myself like Bruno. Or taking my clothes off like Maria. Or snipping all the flowerheads off with my nail scissors. There is nothing wrong with me, I tell you, except my dreams.

They are very spooky, I'll admit that. That's why I consented to go to the clinic at all. I wake up screaming in the middle of the night, hot all over. Then I can't go back to sleep. They tried all sorts of pills, tranquillisers, stabilisers, injections, the lot. I took the pills all right, didn't have much choice. Mummie watched me swallowing them. No good at all. My little mummie had to think of something else. She ships me off to that place every other evening. To have treatment. Treatment? I ask you. Talk talk talk, that's my treatment. Actually I don't dislike the talks all that much. He hasn't a clue as to what I've got of course, old Brocky. Dr. Magnus Brockhuus. He's Dutch, I think. Or Swedish or something.

I go into his room. The first thing I see is that awful picture. It's got a shiny metal frame, a couple of red squiggles bouncing across three black squares and a huge yellow dot in the middle. Stupid picture—does not *mean* anything. It's been put there to make you feel small, to get the better of you before you have even started. The walls are white and there's a big bay window without any curtains. I like that. The light streams in and when the trees in the garden move you can see their shadows dancing on the white walls. A thick blue carpet. A little table with a telephone and vase. My straight backed chair and his leather armchair. An old wooden chest in the corner, nicely carved. The room suits him somehow, although I'm a bit jealous of his deep, comfortable chair. I find him sitting in it as usual. His back to the light. Oh, I know. He doesn't want to be seen, but he watches me like a hawk. I don't give anything away, though. What could I give away then? I'm just keeping myself under control, that's all. He is very polite, very well spoken. "Good evening Evalore," he says, "come and sit down. Make yourself comfortable." Then: "A cigarette?" Cigarette, my foot. I'm not allowed to smoke, he knows that. And it's not healthy either. "No, thank you," I say, "but I'd like a drink." That'll teach him. But the old fox goes to a little chest in a corner and brings out a bottle and two glasses. Ballantine's finest Scotch Whisky. A red seal at the bottom and two little upright horses on the label, each holding a flag. I don't believe it. He pours the whisky, tops it up with water and gives me a glass. It doesn't smell nice at all. I take a little sip and put it down. It tastes even worse than it smells. "Don't you like it?" Brocky asks.

"Oh I do, I do, very much—but I'll drink it slowly." Actually it nearly choked me. It burnt my throat like a red hot iron. I won't have another drop. I give it an unobtrusive little kick with my elbow—like that—and oh! what a pity, it spilled all over my nice orange dress. "Here," Brocky says, "let me—" He takes out a big white hanky and rubs the spot off, just at the hem. He gets a good look at my legs. I don't mind, they are quite pretty, nice and long, not children's legs at all, I really am proud of them. Not like mummie's—all short and thin. None of your matchsticks for me. Well shaped too. He can look all he likes. Nothing wrong with them.

We both settle down again. He gets me going. I don't know how he does it. He always gets me going. He simply puts a question, a harmless innocent little question. And I get caught.

"Did you have a nice day at school?"

"Schooldays can't possibly be nice, so why do you ask?"

"But lots of girls like school."

"I'm not . . . lots of girls."

"Who are you?"

That is a stupid question. That is the silliest question ever. He knows damn well who I am. I'll tell him—straight.

"Well, let me see: I am Evalore, thirteen years

old, I live in London, England, I never do my
homework and I don't smoke cigarettes. I come to
see you every other day because mummie and Illo
think it's good for me. Any more?"

Yes. He wants a lot more. He is not all that keen
on my answer.

"Why do they think it's good for you?"

Silence.

"Do you think it's good for you?"

"No. I think it's bad for me. I think a place like
this makes you feel very . . . very inadequate."
(Lovely word).

"How can a place make you feel something different from what you are?"

"I tell you how. I come in here, in the waiting
room, I see all these miseries creeping around, waiting for the knife . . ."

"Knife?"

"*You* know what I mean. Knife in a manner of
speaking. A mindknife."

"Did you make that up? It's a very good phrase."

"Yes, I made it up just now. I'm not a fool, you
know. I can make up words, or destroy words, I
can play about with them. I can make a mummie
come alive or I can kill a mummie . . . a mummie
is dead anyway, isn't she, isn't she?"

"Is she?"

"Yes!" I am jumping up. "She's dead, dead and
buried and somebody dug her out, unwrapped her
and there's nothing inside but dust . . ." See?

Caught me again. I do not know why I get all steamed up.

"Dust," repeats Magnus the Magnificent, as if he had found profound wisdom in my words. "Why dust?"

"Bones too, I suppose, or a skeleton."

This doesn't seem to impress him. I'll lay it on a bit thicker. But he doesn't give me a chance.

"Egypt," he says dreamily, "I've always wanted to go on an expedition . . ." He crosses his legs and says quite casually: "What did you do yesterday evening?"

I was ready for that one. "I listened at the door while they were both talking. They were at it for quite a while, so there was a lot to listen to. I heard every word, every single word."

"Yes?"

What does he mean: yes. Can't he express himself properly. Does he mean "Yes," like all right, or does he mean he wants to know what they said, or what? "If my memory does not fail me," I say in a very adult tone, quite composed it sounds, "I recall them discussing for the hundred millionth time how their life went wrong and why it wasn't their fault." I pause here, to hear what Foxie has to say to that.

He doesn't say anything. He's waiting. Right. The curtain goes up and here is what they said:

"Illo: 'Eva,' he says—stupid to be called Evalore when one's mum is Eva, but then she just hasn't got much imagination—'Eva! Listen to me, *listen* to me. If I'd been in my own country . . .' " I must interrupt here, dearest Foxie. The scene will go on in a minute.

"Dr. Brockhuus," I say to the silhouette in the armchair, "do you know that I am actually sick of hearing them speak like that, do you know that I hate their very guts, excuses, excuses . . . How Illo would have been Prime Minister and mummie would have got the Nobel prize for her wretched stories. Her stories stink, if you don't mind. *Es stinkt,* as they could have said in their country back home."

I am jumping up again and do a little dance: "My mummie is a foreigner, my mummie is a foreigner, a bleeding bloody foreigner." I am spinning like a top, knocking his ashtray over on the nice blue carpet. No reaction. I can do better than that. I do enjoy hating her, in fact it gives me something to think about when I get depressed. Hate is lovely, it's better than your Ballantine—it really *is*, refreshing, and clean, cleaner than anything I know. It's like a shot in the arm. It makes me feel marvellous, I hope I will never stop. I'm spinning like mad . . . stumble over a chairleg and get picked up by His Majesty. He grips my arm and puts me firmly back on my chair.

"You hurt me," I say whimpering, "you hurt me terribly. My arm is bruised, look it's all blue . . ." He's taken his glasses off and looks at my bare arm.

Turns it round, can't find a mark. His eyes are the same colour as Illo's, dark, with a lovely sparkle. But his face is very different. Illo's is more settled—no, that's not the word I want—more robust, sterner. His is so pale and fragile, with deep creases on his forehead and down to his mouth on either side of the nose. He does not look sad though. But there is something odd about him, which I can't name, something mysterious and hidden. Maybe it's because his hair is almost the same colour as his skin—pale, silvery grey. It's hard to tell where one starts and the other finishes. As if he'd stepped straight out of a ghost story. *That's* it! He looks haunted! Perhaps that's why he wears specs all the time. Bet he just hides behind them. He's got nice hands, though. I liked him touching my arm. He sits down again, crossing his legs and says calmly: "I know you don't like your mother all that much, but your father—I thought you got on well."

That was the longest sentence to date.

"Of course we get on well. It's just that I can't stand them talking about their past."

"Why?"

Why, why, why, do I have to have a reason for everything? How stupid! I haven't got a reason, or wait—maybe I have: "Because Illo gets dragged down by these talks. He shouldn't complain, he's so . . . marvellous, he shouldn't whine about how he could have been, he *is* . . . he's important, he's clever, he's good, far too good for . . . some people . . ."

"The scene you were describing . . ."

I've calmed down. I like descriptions. My essays and compositions are not at all bad. "Yes. They were sitting by the window—I've hidden all the keys and I love peering through the holes. Does she have to sit with the sun shining on her hair? She does it on purpose, of course: it goes all soft and glowing—and Illo said: "You made me come here. I never had a chance, I have no scope, I could have done much better in the States; they would have appreciated . . ."

" 'Yes,' she says meekly, 'I know. I often blame myself.' The snake, the bloody snake. She hasn't blamed herself for anything since she was born. She lowers her head a little, looks at him with those painted eyes, can't think why he lets her paint them like a tart, and goes on: 'Perhaps, if you'd started your studies all over again here, it might have been different . . .'

"I'll say it would have been different. Why didn't he? Why didn't he? Because she went and got herself pregnant. *Pregnant.* Expectant, if you prefer."

"So," says Magnus, "that must have been well over thirteen years ago."

That was a matter of fact statement. But for some reason it drives me hopping mad. "Thirteen years ago—thirteen years ago," I ape his voice, "it was not, you don't know, it was *not*—it was twenty years ago! Not me, do you hear, it wasn't ME, it wasn't me . . ."

A vase filled with gorgeous red roses stands by the side of the armchair. The whole room smells of them. What an innocent sweet smell. I am whipping them out, all fresh and dripping with water and throw them on the floor, stamping on them as hard as I can. The crushed petals make big red spots on the blue carpet. I am stamping on them with both feet, hard, hard. What a lovely mess, leaves, thorns, buds, all squashed.

"It was not me, it was not me, it was the baby, the dear little baby, the dead baby, the weak baby, it couldn't live, they had it in an oxygen tent and all, but it was weak, weak, with a bad heart, three weeks old and died, not like me, fat and full of, full of . . ." I am crying now, "I am only a substitute, they never wanted me, they wanted this baby, I'm a *replacement*, do you hear, a replacement!" I am getting mad at the roses again, squashing them to pulp. That's right, to pulp, all gone. I take the vase and send it hurling against the wall. Splinters fly in all directions, the water makes a nice big spot on the wall.

I am screaming now: "Did you get it, did you take that in, *Doctor,* did you? It was not me she carried around in her big drum of a tummy, waddling along like a duck, oh, I've seen them shuffling along the street with their bellies sticking out, I wasn't there . . ."

"Where were you then?" he says. Just like that. No reference to the flowers or the smashed vase or my goings on. That flooded me.

"Where was I?" I repeat stupidly. What does he mean "where was I?" "When I'm not born I can't be anywhere, or . . ."

"You don't just materialize out of thin air," he says quite seriously. "There must have been something there. What was it?"

I'm speechless. He must be unhinged. I've finally done it. I've driven him round the twist. But he doesn't look mad at all. In fact, he takes his glasses off, polishes them and puts them back on. "Something there before . . . before I was born, you mean?"

"Yes, that's what I mean. Think about it." He gets up, to indicate that the session is over. I don't want to go. I wish he would take his glasses off again, so that I can see his eyes. But he opens the door, gives me a gentle shove and I'm out in the passage. "See you Wednesday at six," he calls after me.

two

AT school next morning. Miss Tuddyfoot for English. Very progressive, Miss Tuddyfoot is. Never raises her voice, reads poetry to us "if we are in the mood," she always asks us politely whether we would like some, or whether we perhaps prefer being "creative" ourselves. Can't stand her high tinny voice, so nice, so cultured, so understanding. "I know what girls are." Girls! She's never been one, I doubt she even has the curse. No breasts to speak of. Mine are coming on nicely, though. For some time I thought there must be something wrong with my mechanism. I stood in front of the glass—mummie's dressing table—and there wasn't even the slightest bulge. No hint of it. Maybe I was meant to be a boy. I'm all right now—that's obvious.

To-day we are going to be creative. Tuddyfoot wears her south-sea beads. "Perhaps," she says sweetly, sounding like a flute with cotton wool down its mouth piece, "perhaps you would want to feel free to do what you like, so I give you forty minutes of freedom. Just let me have a nice piece of creative writing at the end of it."

I feel free to do what I like. I like to burn that school down, that horrid school with its dingy green walls and hard narrow benches. They are too low anyway, made for girls with short legs and fat bums so that they won't feel how hard the wood is. This sickly green colour gets on my nerves, it's everywhere: in the passages, on the doors, even on the window frames. And those high narrow windows—like a prison. The headmistress says it's for safety reasons. I know *her* reasons: she's mean! Won't let us look out on the road for fear we might miss a few precious words from the teachers. Mean and stingy as her small windows and shabby blackboards,

Feel free, Tuddyfoot said. In that rathole? How can I possibly be free? I'd like to burn that school down. Free my . . . *cul!* I'm settling down wondering what to do with my freedom, when Magnus's face floats into my mind: where were you then, where . . . You don't materialize out of thin air, that's true. There must have been something there . . . I begin to write.

"I was everywhere at once. I was in the trees in the clouds in the rain and in the river. My voice was the voice of the wind but I had no thoughts, no need of thoughts, I was not going anywhere so I had no need to think, but I felt everything between

heaven and earth and above moving along with the
stars I was cool as the moon and burning like the
sun and no shape would spoil and force me to show
myself ever . . ."

"Evalore has a good imagination but she should
take more care of her commas and full stops."
Balls! I do what I like. If I'm given freedom . . .
She never meant it, of course, silly old Tuddy, silly
Toad. Some girls think her great though. Mummie
thinks the world of her. Illo said: "Her nose is too
pointed—it's disturbing." He was right there. She
could pick up the litter in the road with that nose
. . . He's marvellous really. I don't know any other
father like him. Now who else would be disturbed
by the shape of a teacher's nose? After all he's been
through, he can make a remark like that. You
would think he'd be a bitter old "Wackelgreis" as
he calls himself. A wobbling old dodderer. I never
mentioned it to Brocky. Will do this afternoon . . .
As I enter his room I quickly look at the carpet.
Clean as a whistle. You wouldn't think there had
been even the shadow of a stain on that lovely
Mediterranean blue.

A new vase stands by his chair. But there are
carnations in it, not roses. "What lovely flowers," I
say to him—I'm no coward—"do they come from
your garden?" Has he got a house, a flat, is he married, children, I haven't a clue. He digs up all about
me, I don't even know how old he is.

"No, from the clinic's garden, I like them just as much as the roses." He's no coward either. "Won't you sit down?"

I shall not sit down, face the light and have his face in the shadow.

"My eyes hurt a little, I do too much work at home." I am saying this in my "honest" little girl voice. "I would be so grateful if you let me move my chair round a little . . . the light . . ."

"Of course," he says, "just be comfortable." I am very, very comfortable. I can watch his face for a change. My feet are squarely on the rug, I'm pulling my dress down and fold my hands in my lap.

"I'd like to speak about Illo," I go on with that truthful voice. "I have to think of him all the time." That's what he wants to hear, doesn't he? That's what they all want to hear. He leans forward a little. Oh, he's in for a very big disappointment, he isn't going to get any girlie feelings at all. Just facts. And ugly ones at that. He is not going to like this one little bit.

"You sit there," I spit at him suddenly, "sit there and worry about my mind, whilst people murder and kill and starve. Don't you *mind*? Is that all you can do? Sit there and listen to people's drivel day after day? His mother . . . her father . . . her grandmother . . . You make me sick! Why don't you go out of that cosy little room and *do* something . . ." I'm quite cool underneath, but I'll keep it up. He does not make a move, but I know I've hit him. I can see his nails digging into his palm. Good!

"You call yourself a doctor? My uncle is a doctor. He *helps* people. When they are ill he gets up in the middle of the night and goes and helps them. Do you get up in the middle of the night? Do you?"

Why do I want to hit him? What's come over me all of a sudden? He has not *done* anything to me. Why does it give me such pleasure to see him digging his nails into his hand? I don't understand. I can't stop myself, I've got to go on . . . "I bet you earn a lot of money just listening to people. Maybe you even like it, maybe you . . . you can't do without it, you need it you NEED it! I know you, you haven't got anything inside, so you take us, us, and fill yourself with it."

I sink back exhausted. I can't even watch him any more. I am tired—I want to go home. "Evalore," he says without raising his voice, "I am *trying* to help, but I have to do it my way. "He looks pale. I did that. I made him look pale. I made him take me seriously. "About Illo," he goes on—he did not say "your father"—"you were going to speak about Illo."

All the fight has gone out of me. I would like to lie down and sleep, just sleep. "He's a brave man," I begin listlessly, "he has gone through terrible things, nightmarish things, and he is never afraid, he always says what he means, he talks to me like a

. . . like a friend. He hasn't got any friends, really, they are not up to much, little Spiessers, the lot of them . . ."

"Little what?"

"Spiessers. You know, sheep, good old doggies who follow their master, people who do like everybody else does, not a thought in their heads." I'm beginning to wake up! I feel more lively now. "All their ideas tidily packed in little compartments, provincial, narrow-minded"—I'm running out of words, then I'm off again—"Even if they lie, they make it a nice lie, if they shout, they control their voices, they don't let themselves go . . ."

"Like you?" Magnus Brockhuus says.

"Yes. Like me. I am only thirteen, but if I lie," I am looking straight into his eyes, "I make it a big decent-sized lie, if I am shouting, I bring the house down . . ."

"Illo," he says gently, "you were saying . . ."

"Yes. He must have had a terrible time. He was born before the war, not the last one, the one before."

"So was I."

Well—you could have knocked me down. He's spoken. He has volunteered some information about himself. I've seen him for months three times a week and he has never ever said a damn thing. He takes me into his confidence. I must be careful. I'm not stupid. He never does anything without a purpose. He wants to make me relax, that's it. "Be comfortable." He won't catch me—I'll watch out! Still, if he too was born before the First War, he must be—he must be about sixty. Sixty. Doesn't look it. But Illo doesn't look "old" either. When do people look old? When they get that defeated sort of look, when they feel that nothing can "happen" any more. I'll never get old. Doesn't matter about their hair really, except for women, that's why they all go to the hairdresser as if he was some sort of medicine man with a secret youth drug. I won't do that, I'll have an accident and no pain, I won't feel anything. Jane says you can tell people's age by their hands. Count the brown spots on the back, add them up, divide them by three and you've got their age. Has he got any? Three on one hand and none on the other. It doesn't seem to work.

"Have you been in the war—fighting?"

"Yes. I was wounded early on." He smiled. "That's why I sit in this chair and don't go round chasing trouble."

Oh God. Oh dear sweet God—what *have* I done? I could just about cut my throat. I wish he would do something horrible to me. I wish he would bash my head in. Or beat me up. I daren't look at him. "Where?" I manage to croak.

"In France," he says.

"No, where . . . where is the scar?"

He is pointing to a spot just over his heart.

"Show me," I say in a very low voice. That is a woman's voice. I am not thirteen. He slowly unbuttons his shirt and shows me a long white scar. I am getting up from my chair, come over to him and touch the scar. It feels quite smooth. It doesn't look ugly. It has become part of him. I am slowly getting back to my chair, feeling most peculiar. That scar. The feel of it. We don't speak. It is as if the air in the room had become dense. It's hard to breathe. He gets up and opens the window.

"Right," he says cheerfully. "The show is over. You said Illo was born before the war . . ."

I am afraid. I can't say why, but I'm stiff with fear. What's the matter with me? Was I scared by the scar? Ha! That's a good one . . . The scar scared me. I'll have to forget about it, won't I? "Yes. Before the war. In Germany, in a big city. It must have been marvellous with lots of theatres and night clubs and everybody earning a lot of money except the poor."

He giggles. He definitely giggles. Have I said something funny? His Majesty has a fit of laughter. "Except the poor," he repeats. "If it wasn't so true it would be ridiculous." He is positively human. He is laughing his head off. "Evalore, you are a baby, an infant," he cries out. "I've never heard such . . ." he goes into convulsions. Now why is he laughing at me? I just wanted to give him the background, fill in the past. He'll be rolling on the floor in a minute. I don't like that at all. I'm not a child. I heard mummie say so the other day. They were leaning out of the window, talking. If I open the kitchen window I can hear every sound. It's like an amplifier.

Just caught mummie's voice: ". . . and I tell you she's slimming. Don't you notice anything? She's stopped biting her nails. Did you see her hands?"

"Yes," says Illo, "she's got nail varnish on. Why do you think she does it?" That's typical, like a man, that is. Because it looks better, that's why.

Mummie: "I am a bit worried—sigh—I know they grow up quicker nowadays—sigh, sigh—but there is something about her . . ." She draws in her breath, then: "She's so—precocious. She doesn't look thirteen, she looks sixteen, and sometimes she . . ." whisper whisper, then, "I've caught her at it . . ."

Illo is annoyed. What could she have said? "Stop it, Eva." He is really angry. "I don't want to hear about it." The bitch! What did she say? Ah, perhaps that I pinch her stockings and put her clothes on. All the girls do that! She has far too many clothes anyway. What's it she wants to dress up for anyway . . . She's got her husband. Or that I'm wearing a bra? No, it can't be that. She told me herself it's better to start early. Oh—I know. She's heard Jane and me talking. Jane said: "You can tell what they look like—you know what I mean—by their faces."

"By their faces?"

"Their noses, silly, same size, same shape."

"How do you know?"

"I just do, you check."

Now I'm looking at noses all the time. Maybe mummie meant that. But then she would have to know too ... she probably does ...

Magnus has stopped laughing and we proceed. That is, I proceed.

"They had a good life." So Illo tells me, lots of friends and they were both students. "Oddly enough I am interested in their past. Nobody else is. They couldn't care less if their parents had been imprisoned. Perhaps because they weren't. Mine were. I am so proud of it. I think it's marvellous. Although they didn't mean to, of course. It was because they couldn't help it, something to do with a political set-up, called Nazis. I am never quite sure what happened. Because whenever Illo starts talking about it, mummie says, I don't want to hear about it—it's gone, it's over; whenever there is a cruel bit on television, she rushes out of the room and I can hear her sobbing in the next room.

"There was a film the other night about Germany and the Nazis and people imprisoned in camps. She wanted to make a bolt for the door, but Illo said: 'You know it all happened, you know it's true—why run?'

"She almost screamed at him. Never saw her like that before: *"Because* it's true, because I saw it, because it goes on all the time all over the world, I cannot bear it ... if you think it's good entertainment, I'm not keeping you.' And she cried and cried. 'This violence,' she kept saying, 'why do people have to hurt each other? This violence, the urge to kill for some stupid idea.' She got more and more excited, I think she forgot there was me and Illo with her. 'It's because their lives are dull and empty and meaningless . . . those fools, those fools . . . They will believe anything as long as it gets them out of the rut.' She stood there in the middle of the room, tears pouring down her face. Then she switched off the television and turned her face to the wall.

"I was frightened. Illo stroked her hair and didn't say anything. He just looked sad and helpless. I watched them both and felt very small, very ignorant. They had seen it all. *I* just know school. I didn't mind Illo stroking her hair. It seemed right. At the time. But why are people so cruel and violent—I'm not like that, am I?"

Magnus just looks at me. "Aren't you?" he says, looking at the carnations and at the wall, where the smashed vase had left a spot on the white wallpaper.

"That's different," I say, "they were only flowers, that doesn't count!"

He draws himself up in his chair and becomes very much the doctor. There is a wall between us all of a sudden.

"Why is it different?"

"Well, flowers are not alive really, they don't feel anything . . ."

"We do not know that for certain. But that's not the point. What made you so mad?"

"I don't remember—I don't remember!"

He doesn't say a thing. He's waiting. One hand is drumming on the arm of his chair. He's looking out of the window. Good profile, if only he had more hair. I do like his profile, he has such a . . . oh, my God. I won't look at his nose. I refuse to look at it. Jane said . . . Damn Jane. Why must she spoil everything. Can't she talk of anything else ever? Perhaps there is nothing else to talk about. Girls and boys, men and women . . .

"Evalore," Mag says, "you do remember," he smiles a little, "big bellies waddling along . . ."

The baby! I feel hot all over. I feel I am going to burst any minute: "That beastly brat!" I am screaming at him again. "No wonder she can't get it out of her mind. It didn't have a chance to show her . . . a girl it was, she *would* have been horrible, she would have bitten her nails, she would have stuck pins into people, and she would have been *ugly,* really ugly with a crooked nose and a squint . . . she would have been old by now, old, at least twenty, and she would never have found a boyfriend, because she's mean, mean and stupid with dirty hair and she would smell, because she never had a wash, people would avoid her like the plague. She hasn't a friend in the whole wide world, not a single friend, because she hates everybody and —and everybody hates her. She's cheating and lying all the time, she steals, you know, she goes into the dressing room at school, and opens all the purses. But she'll never own up of course, oh no, not she. She loves other people getting the rap . . . A real beast, I tell you, she'll murder somebody, quite soon, you'll see, it'll be all over the papers, young girl of thirteen . . ." I'm stopping dead. Mag draws his breath in sharply.

"Thirteen?"

"Did I say thirteen? I mean twenty. She is twenty, or would have been. If she had lived. But they could not make her live. They tried everything. Her heart . . . I haven't got a weak heart. I'm strong, strong, I'll have a marvellous life, I'll do everything she couldn't do, I'll have all the friends in the world, I'll be beautiful, clean and beautiful with lovely hair, clean, clean . . ."

"How did she die?"

This time I open the window. It's so hot, I don't get any air.

"I can't talk here," I say to Mag. "It's not a good place to talk in. Let's go out . . . I'll be able to talk better, I'll feel freer." I see him hesitating and go all out for it: "The room oppresses me, don't you feel it, all the people who have been here before with you . . . They must have poured out such filth. Please take me out . . . I'm so, so"—what is this word they use all the time—"inhibited."

Mag smiles, shaking his head. "I can't do that."

"Can't? Why can't you? Are you not a free man?

After all, it's your clinic. Nobody is going to know about it. And—even if they do? What of it?"

He puts his finger on his left cheek and looks to the window. I'm pushing on. It seems the most urgent thing to get him out of here. I really want to talk.

"This is my place of work."

"That's rubbish. You can 'work' anywhere. You'll see, you can work better somewhere else. And I can talk, oh, how I will be able to *talk*!"

He paces up and down in the little room, trying to cope. I'll cope. I'll make him . . . I am not quite sure why it's so important to me to leave this room with him. But I never wanted anything as much as that.

"Dr. Brockhuus," I am saying, "you are afraid. *You* are afraid." That was a clever thing to say. I know he hates cowards. I'll pursue this line. He still goes up and down, stroking his left cheek. He does not look at me, for the first time in months he does not look at me. I think I'm right. He is afraid. Good. That's a change. I see Jane's grin before me: "Has he tried to rape you yet?"

"I won't rape you," I say aloud. I wouldn't know how, anyway. Can one rape a man?

"That's enough," he snaps at me. "Come on."

three

I go down the stairs with him in a haze. My legs are a bit wobbly. I watch him make an entry in a big open book by the clinic's exit. I have a quick look: "Outing" it says. "Dr. Brockhuus—Evalore. 6:30 p.m. Destination: Regent's Park. Duration: 60 mins," and his signature.

His car is very big and a little old-fashioned, not as sleek as ours. I feel quite timid now that I've got what I wanted. He holds the car door open politely and closes it with a bang after I've sat down. How large the seats are. They are very hot and burn through my summer dress. He gets behind the wheel and we are off. I like the way he drives. Automatically—as he breathes. But very aware of the traffic, he never misses a thing.

Never burns the lights either like Illo. I'm always a little afraid when Illo drives. He's so selfish, he takes no notice of the other drivers. No, that's not selfish, he's just quicker, that's all. We arrive at the

Park and he slows down the car in a road lined with trees. We have only been driving for five minutes or so. Then we pass under a golden gate—Golden Gate, that's good that is—and he pulls up by some building. It's a school, I think, or a college. We are parked in a lonely spot right under some large, leafy trees. It could be miles away right out in the country. A slight haze is drifting over the lawns and bushes which makes me feel very secret and secluded. I'm alone with him—truly alone for the first time.

He leans back and says: "Well?"

Just one word, well. He could have asked me whether I liked the place or something. After all I didn't force him to come here, did I? It's not polite, when one takes out a girl, just to say: well? But then—he is not taking a girl out, is he? I'm his patient. Patient, you blockhead. This isn't John or greedy George with his horrid red fumbling hands. This is your *doctor*. And he wants one thing only: Talk! All right then—I'll talk . . . I'll talk till I'm blue in the face. He tooks straight ahead. I'm waiting for him to turn round so that I can speak to him properly. How can you speak to a person who is not looking at you?

"I'm not a record player, you know," I say angrily. "Why don't you look at me?"

He turns round, takes off his specs, lowers his head a little and smiles right into my eyes. A very nice, kind gentle smile. I feel a sharp pain and my heart contracts like a fist. I must be nuts. There is this nice smile and my heart hurts like hell. What's the matter with me? That old crock smiles at me just to make me talk, not because he likes to sit here. But Evalore isn't a child, oh no, far from it. I won't be smiled at like that. I'm a person, I'm serious, I've got lots of things to give, lots of things to give, lots of things to say, I mean . . . he wants me to say them . . . he wants to hear, doesn't he? It's his job to listen. I'll talk all right, but I'll talk how and when I like. I'm sliding along the seat like a cat and put my head on his shoulder. There. He goes all stiff and rigid. I think he's stopped breathing. I'm squinting up at him. He's gone quite pale.

He isn't exactly a picture of health at the best of times. Not like Illo, who's got a lovely skin, brown in the summer, and olive in the winter. I've never seen such good skin on anybody. Smooth too, and warm. I bet old Brocky's is as cold as death. I catch hold of one of his hands. It *is* cold. It's a large hand, I can put both mine into it. He closes his fingers over them as carefully as if he were holding a couple of raw eggs.

My head on his shoulder, our bodies so close you couldn't pass a thread between them, I start talking. Can't stop. It spills out madly . . . The sun goes down in a red glow between the trees, the park is deserted. He is still sitting next to me. I think he is scared stiff. Why? Why is he scared? Is it that people can see us? What of it? We're not *doing*

anything. No, no. It's not that. Anyway it's so dark
by now, that nobody could see a thing in this car.
He can't be scared of me, can he? Me, a little girl
of thirteen? I am little, even if I pretend otherwise.
I'm nothing—as yet. But some day . . . some day
. . . I'll set the world on fire.

"The baby—" I am saying. "I heard mummie
say it was all her fault. She wanted the baby only as
a protection. This didn't make sense to me. You
protect yourself *not* to have a baby. But you never
know with their generation. But then it became
clearer. There were some idiotic laws in that country where they lived at the time. I think it was
France, the South, somewhere near the mountains.
France had a foreign government, and everybody
who was against it was taken away and killed. But
if a woman was pregnant, then they would not take
her. That was the protection.

"So mummie got Illo to give her a baby. I know
all about it. We have it at school, twice a week. Old
Tuddyfoot. You should hear her: 'The ovaries are
right and left of the uterus and are connected by
the so-called Fallopian tubes to it.' It's a scream.
When she says 'so-called Fallopian tubes' she purses
her lips and goes all neutral as if she was giving a
geographical description. 'The ovaries contain millions of egg cells and when they meet with the male
cell . . .' She keeps up the geographical lark, as if
she were describing a map. 'When they meet with
the male cell the eggs become fertilized . . .' It's

Agriculture now. Tuddyfoot quickly finishes. 'A baby results . . . after nine months. If the egg is not fertilized, the ovum or egg is got rid of at the next . . .' 'Curse' scream the class. 'Menstrual period' finishes Tuddy with dignity. Jane: 'Oh, Miss Tuddyfoot, I can't imagine how the sperm got in . . . I so want a baby, what would I have to do?' Then the class breaks out into a sing song. 'Jane wants a baby, Jane wants a baby, how will she get a baby?' Jane gets up and asks timidly: 'Miss Tuddyfoot, can you explain some of these words, everybody seems to use them, and I feel so stupid . . .' and she comes out with all the words from the Piccadilly lavatories whilst the girls are choking. Poor old Tuddy, she's got a handful.

"So—Illo gave her a baby. She knew right away, she says, she had a feeling after the second day that her body had changed, I wonder what she felt. I also wonder why Illo did it. It It It, yes, he did it, didn't he. I can't imagine him . . ."

"Don't!" Mag says so low that I can't be sure he said anything. Without moving my head from his shoulder I look at his face. He is still staring straight in front. As rigid as a statue. Maybe he's dead. Or he's come back from the dead like the statue in *Don Giovanni*. "You," I don't know what to call him, "you . . . are you listening to me? It's like talking to a brick wall." Ah, he stirs a little.

"Brick walls can be very comforting," he tells me.

I clasp his hand a little tighter. "For comfort," I say. What nice hands he has. Illo's are much nicer, of course. Still—his are very pleasant. If he takes his hand away I'll stop talking. If he moves an inch, I'll stop talking. He's put me off now with his "don't!" Why shouldn't I? Why shouldn't I talk about Illo making love to my mother—it's legal. It's normal. Perhaps my talking about it isn't!

But I'm ill, under medical care, in a clinic, I'm a nut, a little brown nut, and they want to crack me . . . he's *got* to crack me or he doesn't know his job. Come on then, have a go! Say something.

Not a word. We've been sitting here for half an hour and all he said was "well" and "don't." That's not much.

"Are you married?" Like a gunshot that came. I did that very well. Like a policeman. Unawares, that's the word—I took him unawares.

"Yes," and just when I thought he won't give me more than one syllable at a time, he says, "I've been married forty years."

Holy Moses! Forty years. That's historical. I just can't imagine that many years.

"Forty," I say disbelievingly.

"I married very young," he goes on, "at nineteen." He volunteered that . . . very generous.

"How many children?"

He is quiet. He goes paler still, if that is possible.

"How many *children?*" I insist, he's *got* to tell me.

"None."

"Didn't you want them?"

"Yes."

"Did they die, like mummie's?"

"No, I . . ."

Ah—ah, that's where the tide turns. That's how the cookie crumbles, that's how the something jumps . . . *He* is thirteen, he is thirteen, I am putting the questions now:

"If you wanted them, why didn't you? Why didn't you have them then? Or perhaps your wife is . . . is sterile? She can't have them . . . is that it? Her tubes don't work, or maybe she hasn't got a uterus . . . I know a girl in my class hasn't. The doctor says so. Isn't that lucky now, she never need spend her money on tampax . . . And she can make love all the time, with anybody, whenever she wants and she'll never never . . ."

He slaps me right across the mouth with his free hand. That's what I call a slap. It hurts like hell. It's marvellous. Blood trickles out of the corner of my mouth, runs down my neck and dyes the V neck of my dress dark red. It's white, my dress, and the red stain spreads slowly like a Japanese paper flower. He looks at it as if he's seeing a ghost. He draws back. He frowns. Speechless.

"May I have a hanky, please," I say quite naturally. "It's my best dress." He still doesn't move. "Spit on it," I hiss, "spit on your hanky and rub out the stain . . . mummie will be angry . . ."

Thirteen! I'm a woman, I can handle him . . .

He takes a hanky out of his pocket, holds it carefully to his lips—he wouldn't do a vulgar thing like spitting—and starts rubbing the red spot. It gets worse, of course, I knew it would.

He's made a right mess there. It'll never come out in the wash. But I don't want it to come out. It won't even go in the wash. I'll keep that dress. It will go into a smart little cellophane bag, and it will stay in my bottom drawer under my woollies. I'll look at it from time to time and I'll think about it . . .

"Better send it to the cleaners, they'll make a better job of it."

"I can't do that"—I am going all timid and embarrassed—"mummie will ask me how it happened . . ."

"You must tell her, of course." I believe he's serious.

"I can't do *that*! I don't want to get you into trouble. 'Doctor beats up girl patient in Regent's Park!' You must be joking . . ."

He does not answer. In fact, he does not speak at all any more. He backs out of the Park, drives to the clinic—didn't take any notice when I asked him to drop me off at the flat—goes straight to the Reception and clocks in. "Return to the Clinic at 7:30." Yap!

He goes past me without a look: "See you Friday at six." The bastard.

four

NOBODY is in when I arrive at the flat. The dress gets tucked away. I'm so hungry. I'm eating everything in sight and have four cups of tea. Mummie says never more than two—it makes me too excited. But I want to get excited. I feel let down. I thought I had him there just then . . . I'll see him the day after to-morrow. It's a long time to wait. I ought to do my essay for once. Perhaps Illo will help me, he's so good at it. As editor of a paper he's got to be able to write, I suppose.

I can't settle down to anything. Strolling through the flat I think for the hundredth time how beautiful it really is. Not like Jane's poky little place. Ours is lovely, special. Covered all through with a sort of rusty red carpet. White walls and touches of blue and lilac and a deep golden brown. Plants everywhere, even in the bathroom. They like the steam, I think, crawling up the wall like ivy. It's all so lively—not "arranged," things just happen to be there and they fit. Old and new all mixed together. There's a Portuguese jug and a Mexican one that must be hundreds of years old and lots of pictures and plates hang on the wall. I like to walk through the rooms and think it's mine, really mine, not hers. If it were mine, I wouldn't change much. Let me see . . . The sun is streaming in, a warm spring sun, shines right on mummie's small desk. The dust! She can't be bothered, as I said. You would think she'd look after such a lovely flat. Oh no, not mum. I've seen her . . . She simply brushes the dust from the top of the floor. Lets it lie there and thinks she's done her good deed for the day. Then she makes two holes in a tin of fruit juice and settles down at her typewriter. She picks up the tin from time to time and pours it straight into her mouth. Madam can't be bothered to get a glass. She is being creative. Madam can't be bothered to put on a pair of shoes. Her fingernails are broken, because she hammers on the machine all the time. Her jumper is torn, because she pulls at it when she can't write.

What does she find to write about, I wonder? All those poems, those stories, where does she get them from? I know: she watches . . . she watches everything and stores it away. Does she ever write about me, or Illo, or any of our friends? We haven't got friends in common, really. Their friends. More like fiends—I can't stick any of them. All gloves and hats and square handbags with a metal strip on top. I hate those bags. Dull looking things. Why can't they have nice fancy ones like my friends, Jane for instance. She has a smashing one with three little pockets right on top of each other. Or Lilia, the glamourpuss. She's got one made of real fur, her father must be lousy with it. Is Illo? Is he lousy with it?

That's odd. I don't know. If anybody asked me, I would not know whether he's rich or not. Mummie doesn't seem to know either. When I ask her whether I can buy a new dress, she always says: ask daddy—I don't know. You can't tell from the way she dresses either. Sometimes, when she goes out, she puts on the most fantastic things and people ask her where she's got them from. I can't remember, she says. I believe it's true. Once I was with her and she saw a coat hanging in a little shop window, she walked in, tried the coat on, hardly bothered to look and said "I'll keep it on. Chuck the old one away." And as an afterthought: "How much is it?" Funny, she never talks about money . . . all the girls tell me their parents quarrel like mad all about money all the time. I believe she doesn't care as long as she can have her mascara. The furthest she ever got to talking about it was when she said: "Illo is there any money in the house, I just can't think what I did with it." I think she puts it on, though. She must know how she spends her money, *her* money phh! It's Illo's money she is spending. Mostly. She doesn't get much for her writing, does she?

It's odd, I hate her very guts, but I like what she writes. She often asks me whether she is using the right expression or how to spell. She can't spell. It's not her fault, she is foreign. I know how to spell. I know all the difficult words, I don't ever have to look them up . . . It's eerie, all alone in this flat. I wish Illo were here. I wouldn't even mind her . . . where is she anyway? Shopping? She doesn't go shopping. She picks up the telephone and reels off a list of things, giggles, says: but Mr. Cooper, where will I put all this? puts the phone down and attends to her eyes, surrounding them with all sorts of muck. Green, black, silver, the lot. Says they are so small, if she wouldn't point them out, people would think she hasn't got any. It's true, they disappear completely when she loves . . . loves? Laughs, I mean, when she is laughing.

I don't know what she does when she loves . . . those two beds tucked up together. Why can't they have a night table in between, like everybody else. It's disgusting, those beds. It's so obvious. It's without . . . without discretion. After all, I am here too in the same flat. Can't be Illo's idea. She makes him do what she wants. She's a real slut. Slut! Slut! What does a slut do? I wish somebody would come home. I don't much like being along. Mummie doesn't seem to mind. I caught her talking to a plant though, when she thought she was alone in the flat. She's bats of course. I always knew that. She said: "Now why do you go yellow in the spring? You're naughty, you mustn't mix up the seasons"—she put her cheek against the leaves—"I'll give you some more water and I'll put you out on the window sill, but you've got to behave . . ." as if it were a baby. Stupid! A grown up person talking to a dumb plant. Plants can't understand—or can they? Brocky said we are not sure they don't feel. How can a plant feel? With what? It hasn't got a mind . . . maybe it feels without a mind, it just—feels.

Ah—there is the door—oh, I hope it's Illo. It must be. His step is much heavier. It is, it is. And she's not here. I hope she never comes, I hope she'll drop—no I don't. I don't. I didn't mean to think that. Forget that I thought . . .

"Oh there you are, that's nice, oh I love that coat."

Illo is wearing a leather coat with a fur collar. Dark brown leather and dark brown fur. I like stroking it, it feels like an animal. "Shall I make you some coffee?" Yes, he would like some. He looks tired. "I'll bring something to eat as well, mummie's not here. I don't know where she can be . . . We don't need her, do we? I'll look after you." He gives me a funny look. I only said I'll look after him.

"Just the coffee, thank you."

Now what have I done. And I was so pleased to see him. Perhaps he's furious that mummie is not home. I place the coffee in front of him on a small Turkish table and settle down by his feet, flinging my arms around his legs. I could sit like that forever. I put my head against his knee and close my eyes.

"Sorry, I'm late—the traffic." She's back. The bitch is back—back is the bitch. Why can't she leave us alone. It was so good, so safe, so lovely.

The moment she enters the room Illo shoos me away like some nasty fly. He looks at her as if he'd never seen her before. She doesn't do too badly, I must admit that—for a mother. It's not that she conceals her age, or dresses young. She's so uncaring. Though not carefree. I've seen her, looking out over the hills, turning to the south—she is always turning to the south when she looks out, I wonder why?—and turning back with both hands hiding her face. Does she cry? For what? For whom? Me?

There she stands with her short brown curls and her pale pink lips. She's very small, I think I'm a little taller even. It's a pity she's my mother. Sometimes I wish she could be my friend. But she is not, is she? She's my bloody mother. Bloody bloody mother . . . does she have to kiss Illo right on the lips when I'm there. He's grinning like he'd just been given an MBE. What is an MBE? People talk about it. I think it's to do with politics. I hate politics. I hate history. It's all about who murders whom and when and where. Why do we have to learn all that rubbish? It doesn't make the slightest difference because it all goes on just the same all over the place. The news! Illo and mummie glued to the set, seeing bodies dragged along, or people being shot. Funny mummie not minding the news and running for it when it's about something that happened twenty-five years ago. Oh I'm tired, I'd like to stop thinking . . .

five

AGAIN: I woke up screaming. Mag said I should write down my dreams at once . . . "I was walking along the beach and it was very cold, cold and windy. The waves, huge waves came rolling in and crashed down on the sand. Seagulls flew past, their ugly beaks wide open. Low grey clouds overhead and red cliffs bordering the sands. Nobody else, just me. I was crying, because somebody had died and I couldn't face the lonely house. Somebody I loved very much, because I kept calling his name again and again. I shall never return to the house, never, never. And I called his name again, softly, many times. Suddenly I heard his voice close to my ear: But I'm here, right next to you, I said I would never leave you. I looked around, my damp hair flying across my face, but I could not see anybody. Where, I called, where are you—I can't see . . . Then the voice came again: Think of me, imagine me, shape me. Maybe the voice came again: Think

of me, imagine me, shape me. Maybe the voice was
in my head. I got quite desperate. Shape me, it said
. . . remember the last time we walked here together, remember—remember . . .

"Suddenly I felt I was leaning against him, my
head on his shoulder, the weight of his arms around
me and there he stood in front of me, but he looked
weak and pale. He was not really standing, he was
hanging between the sky and the earth. I called him
again, louder and stronger. He came closer, he was
more real, more alive. He stretched out his arms,
coming nearer, wanting to touch me . . . I couldn't
let him . . . dead people can't touch you . . . you
die if they touch you—I started screaming—"

That's when I woke up. Can't make head or tail
of it. Maybe Brocky can. I'll take the sheet of paper
with me and read it aloud—he won't be able to understand my scribble . . .

That's the limit! For once I was really glad to
talk to Brocky and they have to butt in. Mummie's
fault again, Illo would never do a thing like that.
That's *my* doctor, *my* clinic, I don't want her to interfere. I saw them sneak in, have a quick word
with the receptionist and go upstairs. But I am
quick too—I raced after them, nobody saw me—
and here they are disappearing into Mag's room.

I've got to, *got* to hear what they say. The room
next to Mag's is empty. Dr. Peterson is not coming
to the clinic to-day. The walls are so thin I bet I can

hear them talking. Tidy room this . . . my ear is pressed to the wall.

". . . It is disturbing" (mummie, of course) "disturbing how much she understands. She ought not to *know* that much. I feel sometimes really uncomfortable, especially when she smiles. Her eyes don't smile, it is as if she had some sort of secret and wants me to know it's there, but . . . but—"

"Yes?"

"She won't tell. Her own mother. And I love her so much, so very much. There's nothing I would not do for her, you know that."

"Do I?" Good old Brocky. Let her have it . . .

"I literally adore her. I know there is this—this thing with my husband, but I understand, I really do, children, girls of her age . . ."

"Children?"

"Well, she *is* a child at thirteen. She hasn't even had (mumble) for very long so she is a child physically. No, I mean she's got it, although I think it's wrong to have it early, but she doesn't *act* as if she had. Running around naked in the flat. That's a bit much, even when I am alone with her, she hasn't any . . . decency . . ."

"What is—a bit much?"

"Her running around like that."

"A child?"

"She doesn't *look* like a child. She just acts like one."

"You just said: she knows too much."

"Oh I don't know. I can't make her out, she confuses me . . ."

"How?"

"I think she hates the very sight of me, always trying to get Illo on her side, when we quarrel."

"Who quarrels?"

"Evalore and I. She's so stupid" (I'll show her who's stupid) "so, so . . . greedy, she never tidies her room, she pinches my clothes, she never does her homework, runs around like a savage with just a couple of rings on her fingers as if she wanted to show . . . she me . . ."

"Go on."

"Doctor Brockhuus" (I'm sure she's got up from her seat) "Doctor Brockhuus, I am not your patient. I don't see why you have to question *me* like this. Why don't you ask my husband. Perhaps he can tell you all you want to know, perhaps he can also tell you why he sits for hours in his room, talking to her. When I come in they look like a couple of thieves disturbed on the job . . . perhaps he'd like to tell you why he never . . ."

She lowered her voice just then. Why he never—what?

"That is untrue" (Illo) "that's completely and utterly untrue, as you well know. Why did you say that? I forbid you to talk like that. It's a lie . . . Doctor, our relationship is perfectly normal, I can assure you."

"I believe you. I really do. Please don't upset yourself."

Damn! I can't hear a thing. Ah, that's better . . .

". . . rather be with your daughter?"

"What did you say?"

"You heard me."

Dead silence. Then Illo starts laughing. He can't stop himself. He is howling. "Me? Me?" He's off again. I can't bear him laughing like that. It makes me bristle all over. "Stop laughing, stop it, do you hear?"

I am charging into the room. My blood is pounding like mad. I hit Illo as hard as I can, then I take that vase with the carnations and have a go at her, at *her* . . . "Stupid" eh? "Savage," she said. I'll *be* savage . . . The vase breaks into a thousand pieces on her head, her hair is soaking and the flowers rain down on her shoulders, she looks so beautiful with her wet hair and her eyes wide open with fear, the flowers slowly falling to the ground; she has no business looking like that, I'll . . .

Brocky slaps my face twice. My blood stops throbbing as he grips my arms and leads me to a chair: "You definitely don't like my flower arrangements," he says.

Illo is rooted to the spot while mummie goes slowly out of the room without a word. "Oh God," Illo murmurs. "Oh God, what now? And we were planning to go to Italy, the three of us, in two days . . . what now, what . . ."

"I don't see," Brocky smiles, "why it would work better in Cornwall. A little upset here and there doesn't do any harm, it clears the air. You'll work it out, I'm sure."

Illo takes me down the stairs. We find mummie sitting in the waiting room, a scarf over her head. The car is outside the clinic. Mummie opens the back door and sits down quietly. I'll have the front seat. Illo switches the radio on, some idiotic symphony. But I don't mind. I feel fine. The noise of that vase cracking on her head. Did the glass cut her, I wonder. I would have noticed.

I can see her in the wing mirror. She is sitting there huddled in a corner and doesn't move. She looks very white. Usually her skin is yellow. People are always asking whether she has a Chinese parent. And those slanting eyes. I think it's possible. Maybe her mother had . . . If only I wasn't so terribly tired. "We'll be home in a minute," Illo says, patting my hand.

I go to bed at once and Illo draws the curtains. "It's only because you laughed at me . . . I didn't mean to—"

He softly closes the door behind him.

SÍX

ITALY is fine. It makes a change. And the hotel— wow! I'm writing to all my friends on the hotel's postcards. Jane's never been abroad. She'll be furious. Brocky also gets a card: "Better than Cornwall, wish you were here. Love E." Sounds very sophisticated. I did not really mean I wish he were here. But people write things like that. I don't miss him one little bit. In fact, I'll persuade mummie and Illo—I don't *need* to go back.

Love the Italian food. They let me drink wine in the evening. I like that. It's dark red and makes me feel marvellous. We are going out nearly every night. I'll live here when I'm grown up. All those colours and the heat. I adore the heat and the deep blue sky and the people. They scream and shout, cheerfully of course, and their chidren are always around, lots of them, all with dark eyes and olive skin. Maybe I'll marry an Italian with bags of money and live in Rome near the Spanish Steps. Or a poor Italian and live behind the station where all the tarts stand around. The other night we sat in a café and those girls were trotting up and down. They weren't really pretty, but I couldn't stop looking at them.

Illo and mummie were jabbering away in Italian to some man from the hotel—I don't know how they do it, wherever we go they speak the language—and I was watching these girls. Jane said there weren't any in England on the streets and you had to ring them up. Just imagine. Oh hallo, can I come round to-night and make love and what does it cost? Jane said . . . How does she know so much, I'd just like to know. Perhaps her sister told her. She is sixteen. I know all the words too, but I'm not always sure what they mean. Jane does. Has she ever . . .? No, I don't think so. She is going out with that horrid man, he's a man, not a boy, and he takes her to meals and cinemas. Then they sit in the car. She lets him kiss her and once she took her bra off. Some bra she has. The size of it. She says the bigger the better. They'll be like water melons by the time she's eighteen.

Look at that girl then. It's one of "them"—I can tell. They sort of wobble all over and their skirts are too tight. Mine are just as short, but they swing. Do they make a lot of money, and don't they mind? All these men—can they say "no" if they want to? And doesn't it hurt?

This is the best ice cream I ever had. "Want another one?" Illo asks me. Isn't he sweet. He notices everything about me. He knows long before mummie when I'm tired. We went sightseeing without mummie the other day. I usually hate it—it bores me. But with him everything comes alive. We sat down on the steps of the Colosseum and he really made me see what happened nearly two thousand years ago. How the gladiators fought the wild animals, where Caesar was sitting. I could almost hear the crowds roaring. Then, while he was still speaking a procession came along. It was dark and they were carrying torches, real burning torches. A priest was singing and they went slowly past us, all dressed in black, with a sort of shuffle. The women had shawls over their heads and long dark skirts. It made me shiver . . . I thought of all the blood being spilt right here, I could almost smell it . . . I could almost see the great beasts jumping, feel their sharp teeth and claws. I cuddled up to Illo asking him to tell me more and more. It was like drinking the dark red wine at night, only better. I was part of everything, of the huge building, of what had happened so long ago, part of Illo, part of the lovely starry sky, part of the soft warm southern wind . . . he didn't treat me like a child. He thought aloud, describing the city, the old Empire, the things I so hate at school. This is how one should learn, I remember thinking, just before I fell asleep on the steps.

I didn't sleep because I was tired. I just had all I

wanted and fell asleep because I was happy. I've
never met anybody like Illo. He has his back to me
and he knows I want another ice cream. Pity he is
my . . . that's a stupid thought. It's great, of course,
I wouldn't know him at all if he weren't—

"Let's dress up and go to the Via Veneto to-
day," Illo says.

"Make yourself pretty, Evalore," mummie says.
"With all those film-people around, you never know
. . ." I don't trust her when she is playful like that.
She doesn't want me to notice what she looks like.
She's been to the hairdresser. She's got another
colour, for God's sake, it's red, her hair is dark red.
What does she want to go and do that for? She says
it goes better with her tan. She sits in the sun for
half an hour and is brown all over. I just come out
in blotches.

And she's bought a dress too. Silky brown to
tone in with her skin and her golden belt—she's up
to something. Is it for Illo? Or the man from the
hotel we went out with the other night? I've never
caught her looking at other men, really looking I
mean. Talking to lots of them, laughing and teasing, but she does not seem interested. She does not
concentrate. Half the time she does not hear what
they say. When I ask her whether she liked them,
she does not know what I'm talking about. "Like?
Like?" she says. "Clods . . . earthbound." I don't
quite get it.

Why does she bother to talk to them, then? I
asked her the other day and she said: "Confirmation, that's all." I think she forgot she was talking to
me and went on. "I just need confirmation for the
days ahead. I've got to be sure. I must be quite sure
of myself, otherwise it won't work . . . if I'm in doubt
it won't work. But I'm not, I'm not—I never
doubted it. I'll get there if I have to . . ." She suddenly stopped, clenching her fist, saying "Sorry, I'm
just rambling . . ." She was lying, of course. She
was not rambling at all. I could tell from the way
her eyes narrowed and glittered.

I don't know her at all. My mother—what does
she think about? What won't work if she is in doubt
and where does she have to get to? Perhaps it's her
writing. Sometimes she sits quite still, lowers her
eyes and looks as if she were listening—listening to
something nobody else can hear. Then she dashes
to the typewriter and begins to hammer on it furiously.

She tears out the sheets again, crumples them
into a ball and chucks them out the window. I've
seen four or five little white paperballs being chased
by the wind over the grass. Then she starts again
and it looks as if she couldn't catch up with herself.
She pounds on the keys so fast, so angrily, with
such energy as if she had to win a race.

What does she need a new dress for? Oh, I give
up. She is only my mother. I'm not really interested. But I don't want to go to the Via Veneto

with them. I'll have a swim in the lovely pool in my
new bikini. John will come and talk to me. He's always staring at me in the dining-room. I know he is
staring at me and not at mummie. He's from London too. He's asked for my address; then he said
could he come and look me up when we are back?
He is eighteen—I must tell Jane. Good looking too
and clever. I don't think he is a "clod." But I don't
really care, I'm like mummie.

Actually I am better than mummie. I can prove
it. When we go out together it's at me the boys are
looking—me with my short skirt and no make-up.
Who wants to see a lot of paint—that's for art galleries. I loathe those galleries they keep dragging
me to. One picture stuck next to another one.
Makes me dizzy. You look, two steps you look
again—another two steps. There's the next
Madonna, or a lot of fat angels or some stilted
creature turning her eyes to heaven.

Why must they all paint the same things? Illo
says it's a big chance for me to see the great paint-
ers, while I'm young. Great or small, it's all the
same to me. It's flat. I want things to jump at me,
to make me cry or laugh or dream. The pictures *I*
adore are the movies—they suck me up into the
screen and I forget I'm sitting in a cinema. Saw one
just before we left. I remember—it was shot in
Rome, just near the Spanish Steps where we are going to-day. The woman was old—about mummie's
age. Still, I could think it was me somehow—pic-

tures do that to me. I can even be a general, or an old man or anybody looming up large in front of me and talking. It's the voices and the music and I can see every detail and what the person is *thinking*. Just look at their eyes and I hear their thoughts.

I'd give a penny for mummie's thoughts. She doesn't like all the men looking at me and not at her.

I've put my shortest skirt on—just for the hell of it. The girls in Italy don't go about like that. It's their religion. I think it's very strict. It tells them what to do and also what they must not do and read and think. Fancy them being told by a vicar how long their skirts should be. Nobody tells me anything. But maybe it makes them feel comfortable. I don't like to be comfortable. In fact I'm quite happy if I feel really *un*-comfortable. Like now for instance. I know I shouldn't go out like that. That's why I do it. It bothers me. It's good feeling bothered—at least I know I'm there . . . That nice boy now—he can't take his eyes off my legs—I know he's following us. Mummie frowns: "Why didn't you put your dress on, Evalore? It's far too hot for a jumper and a skirt . . ." She couldn't care less about my being too warm. It's my nice long legs she objects to. She's wearing flat-heeled sandals and skirts down to her knees—there is nothing to see. She is too old anyhow—no boy would give her a second look. Maybe an old man . . . She always says that she doesn't like young men and never has. I don't believe a word. They just don't go for her, that's all. I know the young boy is still behind us, hope he goes on that nice old-fashioned tram with us.

He does. He's waiting at the stop and he stands so close to me I can feel his breath. Oho—I can feel something else—his hand, is he trying to—ouch! He's done it. I'm rubbing my bottom, but it doesn't hurt really—that's part of the sightseeing. Many girls go to Italy just for that. Women too. A bit stupid really, any boy in England could do the same. But they don't. Still—to go all this way just to get a blue spot on your *derriere* . . . I've got mine now—my Italian visa . . .

We are sitting in the tram with wooden seats. Not very comfortable and a bit hard if you have nothing to sit on but your skin. The cheek! He is sitting down right opposite. Mummie hasn't realized what's going on—I'm sure she would change seats immediately if she had. I let her sit by the window so she can see all the sights—so can the boy. Lovely eyes, what I can see of them. Because he keeps them screwed to my skirt. But he's seen it all, it won't go any higher. Unless I make it . . . I'm crossing my legs and it rides up. His eyes are popping out. Has he never seen a girl before? I think he likes my white skin, he isn't used to it. He is swallowing hard and licking his lips as if he wanted to eat me. At least somebody likes me. Somebody thinks I'm worth while looking at.

Mummie still hasn't noticed. All those crumbling old houses are far more interesting for her than me. I want her to notice—there's no fun if she doesn't. Then she'll see that—that she is *out! Out!* Mummie is not in the running any more. She can do what she pleases, buy more dresses, have her hair done, slap on the make-up . . . it won't help. She's had it. It's over for you, mummie, you don't count, don't you see?

She doesn't because her head is turned away from me and she sighs from time to time and murmurs: so beautiful, what a city . . . She should look at her daughter. That's far more important than any ghastly old buildings.

The young Italian is leaning forward, he's going to fall over in a minute. His face is sweaty—I don't think he looks all that nice. Oh, now he stretches out his hand and places it right on my knee. I don't like that at all—I don't know him . . . He can't touch me just like that. But I don't budge—mummie will—She must have caught the movement of his hand because she's turned round and is literally screaming at him in Italian. All I can make out is "Thirteen, thirteen" and "mamma"—

That's what I call a good time. She livid. That's really got her, my mamma. She can't stop yelling. It's not only because of the boy, because he scuttled out of the tram as fast as he could once mummie started going for him. She keeps on because she is, she is—frustrated. She wouldn't have minded if the

boy had done it to her. She would have sent her
meaningful little glances all around to say, see, I've
got a big daughter, but nobody is interested in her
. . . They are all shouting together now, the ticket
collector who stands in the middle and all the other
passengers. Mummie lets fly, screeching with the
rest of them. She doesn't look furious any more at
all—she's enjoying herself! At the top of her voice
. . . like a fishwife. My nice refined delicate mummie, with her hands on her hips, yelling . . . Maybe
she is yelling underneath all the time. That's what
she is really like—a shrieking, bawling fishwife—
only in England she doesn't dare.

The whole hullabaloo dies down as quickly as it
started. By the time we leave the tram, mummie has
quietened down completely and just says: "What's
all the fuss about? Why did they get so upset?" I'm
beginning to think I don't know my mamma very
well.

I'm still thinking it. right here on the Spanish
Steps. That's the place for me. All young people—
sitting around with guitars and bottles, speaking every language under the sun, drifting from one
group to another, some without shoes, I love that. I
wish mummie would let me . . . That's the bloody
limit. She's taken off hers, sits down on the steps,
stretches her legs and says: "God—what a place,
I'll stay here for good." She starts talking to a chap
next to her, who is so drunk he doesn't know what
he is doing. How else would he come to giggle his

head off with mummie. And I thought she would get the willies seeing people lounging about on the floor, all dirty and covered with paper bags and food stuff . . . But *la mamma* is on top of the world. She's having the time of her life with that lousy little creep.

Why do they have to speak in French, I can't follow . . . or very little of it. This is *my* outing, we came here because I wanted it, as a special concession to me. Illo is off to another Gallery, the Villa Borghese, I think, and mummie said she would go with me so that I could have some fun. Some fun! She just talks to people she likes and never stops to ask herself whether they like it too. What can they find to talk about? They've never seen each other before. Now he offers her a drink from the bottle.

It's filthy that bottle, I wouldn't go near it. But she pours the wine right down her throat as if she'd done nothing else all her life. And at home she wouldn't touch a drop of anything but her mucky dandelion coffee. I always knew she was sly, sly and crafty . . . I'll see that Illo knows about that. My mother sitting with that—that clown knocking it back, wriggling her toes . . . She writes something on a piece of paper and hands it over to him with a wink. Bitch—bitch! And when she is with Illo she pretends she never looks at another man. I bet she gave him our address. Maybe they'll meet secretly and—"Evalore, it's about time we left . . . oh that's my daughter . . . meet Maurice." The creep looks right through me, says "Mademoiselle" and puts his dirty little paw on mummy's hair. Could be her son, he is so young—except that he wouldn't be so dirty, she would make him wash his feet for a change. And she carrying on in the tram only because the boy put his hand on my knee—hypocrite, liar . . . Yes, Illo *is* going to hear about this, I'll see to that!

"Did you have a good time?" I'm going to tell him what kind of a time we had.

"Great," says mummie, "we met a nice young man, a Frenchman—he's coming to visit us here in the hotel." Hate her more than ever. I can't say anything now. She is too cunning for me. She's spoiled it all.

seven

I don't like Naples at all. Except for the washing hanging out in the streets. All they seem to want is children. They are all over the place. And those big fat women with brats crying and laughing and shouting and not taking any notice of us. As if we didn't belong. They sit out on the pavement, the kids crawling all over them and you can't tell the families apart. Maybe they are all one family. They look alike anyway, and they scream from one house to the other, it must be very funny, because they are shaking with laughter. What have they got to laugh about? They are in rags and most of the kids don't even wear shoes . . . What's so funny about that? They are so—sloppy, I hate that.

I notice I'm doing a lot of hating lately. Not only people but things as well. I hate some colours and shapes, even sounds, especially voices. It might mean that I'm growing up because I'm noticing more of my surroundings. Brocky says, when you hate you envy. That's a load of crap. How could I possibly envy them. Bet they have never been to London. They might never even have been on Vesuvius. We are going there this afternoon.

Illo has hired a car and we are now driving up the mountain slope. He says he does not need a guide, he prefers to use his own eyes. It took ages to get out of the town. Once we nearly ran over one of those kids. Why don't their mothers watch them if they love them so much? Maybe it doesn't matter——they have a new one every year. It's because they are catholic, mummie says. What's Religion got to do with having kids, I'd like to know.

The mountain looks grim. There is nothing growing, not a single blade of grass. We can't go any further up by car. We leave it on a sort of platform and now we are going up on the chairlift right to the top. It doesn't look very safe to me, but nobody has ever fallen out, Illo says, so it must be all right. There are always two seats together, hanging from a cable. I'd like to sit with Illo, all alone just the two of us. But he says mummie is afraid and he doesn't want me to go all by myself, so we are now trying to jump into the seats quickly. There is a man fixing an iron bar on each seat so we can't fall out and up we go.

Oh, this is lovely. No, it's more than lovely it's marvellous, like flying on your own, without a machine. And you can look as far as the sea. Naples is in the distance and the land glitters and shimmers in the heat. I wish we'd never stop. It's quiet. It's so quiet you can almost hear it. It becomes a . . . thing, this silence. It's everywhere, it surrounds us like a soft cloth. There are not even any birds around. It's too high up, or maybe they don't know where to build their nests. There is nothing to feed on, no greenery, just the black stony lava underneath.

I'm enjoying this. Is mummie? I'm watching her in her little cage next to mine. She doesn't seem to know I'm there. She's got her secret face on. Wide open eyes dreaming of God knows what. Her curls are shining in the sun. Her red curls. And look at her hand clutching the bar, it's ugly with its broken nails. She would not even notice if I slipped out of my seat and went crashing down on the black stones, she would just fly on to the top. Never even a look. Only on arrival would she notice that I'm no longer there. And she would go all white like that time in the car, after I'd broken the vase. Then she'd be sorry, then she'd be sorry . . . "Where is Evalore?" Illo would say, and she wouldn't know what to answer. She's say something stupid, like "but she was next to me, I didn't notice . . ." Illo would scream at her and blame her for everything. "Your fault," he would say, "your fault! If she had gone with me nothing would have happened."

They'd shout and shout and the police would come and find out and they'd all blame it on mummie . . . and then, then she'd have him all to herself forever and ever, if only I lifted the little iron bar . . . that's all, and slipped out . . . I'm getting all hot and flushed and excited. It must be the thin air, we are up so high, so alone. Alone! We *are* alone. Nobody would know. Nobody would see anything. It would look like an accident . . . if only I lifted the little iron bar and gave her a little—then *she* would go crashing down on the stones, her red curls on the black stones . . . It's easy. She wouldn't notice for she'd be dead and I would be free. I would cook for Illo and I'd keep the flat *clean,* I'd do my homework every day and we would have such a lovely life, such a good life, nobody to disturb us, and I wouldn't have to go to the clinic any more, I'd spend all my evenings at home with him . . . How does one lift the bar—I'll try it out on mine first. It comes off, oh, it's easy, I'll . . .

"Are you out of your mind?" Mummie pushes the bar down with a bang. "Do you want to fall out? You must be mad! At this height?" She looks down and shakes herself like a dog coming out of the water. She is so frightened she goes on screaming: "I shouldn't have brought you in the first place. It was Illo who insisted . . . I know children shouldn't come on holidays with their parents. We don't get a rest, do we? And you should be with girls of your own age, in a Youth Hostel . . . Why ever did I agree? Well, this is the last time . . ."

She goes on raging like this till we arrive at the little station on top. We jump down from the lift.

As soon as we are standing on our feet mummie gives me a slap, a very hard slap on my bottom. "That's for fiddling around," she says. I don't mind, oddly enough, although people are looking at us. She is quite right, I shouldn't have touched that bar at all. It was a silly thing to do.

Illo is waiting at the top and asks whether we had a lovely ride. Mummie hesitates just for a second, then she says: "Yes, yes, it was great. Did you enjoy yours?" But when Illo wants to take us over the crater, she does not come with us. The two of us go by ourselves. Mummie says she'll only get dizzy on the catwalk.

That's a good word, "catwalk." Because the ridge we are crossing is just wide enough for a cat to walk on in comfort. Illo is walking in front and I'm holding on to his hand. "Don't look down," he calls back to me, without turning his head, "look straight ahead and you'll be all right!"

The walk widens after a few minutes and now we are standing right on the rim of the crater. It's enormous, you can hardly see the far edge of it. You could sink a whole town in this hole. Illo is still holding my hand and we are carefully going down the slope into it. It's fantastic! Hot steam is hissing out from the stones and one mustn't go too near or it'll burn you to cinders. I am not afraid at all. With him holding my hands, I'll never be afraid, I'll go down to hell with him. This rather looks like it— wonder whether there really is a hell or a heaven.

There ought to be. Otherwise people wouldn't behave themselves. They could kill and do all sorts of terrible things and they wouldn't be punished once they are dead. But if they are dead—would they feel they are being punished? I mean how would they know if they can't think about it?

Can you think when you are dead? And if *you* are dead, who can think—it's too complicated. I'll ask Brocky about it, when we get back. There was a book on his desk called *The Book of the Dead*. It was from Tibet, I think. Or India. They think a lot about death in those countries. We don't talk about it much. There is no point to it, is there? When I'm alive I don't need to and when I'm not, I can't think . . .

Miss Tuddyfoot would say: "Evalore, you are being morbid again." Tuddy-my-foot, I won't see her for weeks. But I will see Brocky. He's not so bad, really, I'm almost looking forward . . . "Illo, how long are we staying here, when are we going home, home to London?" I ask.

"What," says Illo, "getting fed up with your old parents already?" We are going back to mummie and this time Illo is riding down with me. He never takes his eyes off me. Why—now why? I didn't hear mummie tell him that I fiddled about with that bar. She must have given him a sign or something. And why can't I fiddle around with it, I'm not a child, I know what I am doing. I wish we were back at the hotel.

The hotel is not half as nice as the one in Rome. It's old and dusty and has no swimming pool and there's veal every day on the menu. What a way to spend a holiday. This morning some ramshackle museum with lots of statues. They stand there and don't move. I know statues don't move, but somebody should make them. And they all look pretty much alike to me. I can't tell one from the other. Mummie says they have a spiritual quality. Spiritual? With everything on show? What's so spiritual about that? Instructive, yes. At least now I know exactly . . . but I still don't understand how they get it *in*. Well, I'll know one day, can't imagine it's going to be much fun though, I'm always wondering what the whole fuss is about.

We are on our way to a church now. A church! That's all I needed. I want to swim, I want the sea and the beach and the countryside. Museums and churches—*pfui*—lovely German word this—*pfui, pfui*, useless, dirty, shameful, horrid, ghastly, it means all that . . . Mummie looks a bit doubtful, because I am wearing such a short skirt. "They might object." Who's they? And why should they object after what I've seen this morning. I am only showing my legs. They are nice and brown by now, I'm using a suntan lotion and they don't go red and patchy.

Here is the church. I'm surprised it's still standing. Crumbling old thing. It's not beautiful at all.

Just because it's old, people go into raptures. There's a man at the entrance who is looking everybody up and down. What for? "No, signorina," he seems angry, he is pointing at my legs. "You see," mummie says, "I told you—he won't let you in because of your skirt!" Illo is discussing it with the old boy, I think he's trying to tell him that I am only thirteen, that I am a child and it does not count—something like that. That's a bit much. I am *not* a child. The old man doesn't believe him anyway. "The man thinks you are fifteen," says mummie crossly. Why should that make her cross. It's nice to look older.

Not for her though, I see that, it makes *her* appear older too. Jolly good. I am not going to be told what to wear by anybody. I am going into this church. The old man tries to stop me, but I'm brushing him aside and just go in. He's coming after me and all the Italians carry on like a lot of flustered hens. "Evalore," mummie is next to me by now, "Evalore, go out at once, I don't want a scandal!"

She doesn't want—well, she's going to get one, right now; I am not leaving this church. Illo tries to reason with me. Says it's not worth it. Well, if it's not worth it, why bother to go there in the first place?

I'm striding forward with the lot of them at my heels like a pack of hounds. What are they yapping about—this morning with all those naked men nobody said anything. On the contrary they couldn't take their eyes off them, I watched some of the girls, and the older women. You would think they'd never seen a man before. They most likely haven't, stupid old spinsters . . . God made them and God made me and my legs. If he didn't want them, all he had to do was to give me a stem like a mushroom. A church! God hasn't built the church, has he? A man built it. They all lie, they all pretend. They are not going to stop me.

The old man from the door is taking me by the arm and literally dragging me out. I didn't think he was that strong. I'm kicking at his shins as hard as I can and he is cursing at me all the time. I don't understand a word and I'm glad I don't know Italian . . . Stupid old bastard, is he getting paid for this? We are nearly out of the church, when I put my foot right between his feet and he falls headlong on the floor and lets go of me. I hope he hurt himself—he must have done, on this hard stone floor. He sits there, dazed, as if he didn't know what had hit him. Mummy and Illo are frogmarching me out into the street and back to the hotel. Nobody says a word.

They are still not speaking to me at lunch. Veal again. I'm beginning to hate this place. When we are up in our rooms I ask mummie when we are leaving. She turns round and looks at me, as if—as if she really hated the sight of me. Her eyes glittering, she slowly advances towards me and grips my throat with both hands. She is trying to choke me. My mother is trying to choke me. Her hands are so tight round my throat I can't breathe. She is hissing and screaming and shaking me like mad . . . I don't defend myself. I just let her . . . Suddenly the pressure of her hands is gone. Illo has thrown her on the bed and leads me gently to my own room and closes the door.

I can hear her sobbing next door. She nearly killed me and I don't mind. On the contrary, I feel much better. I don't resent it the least little bit. That's odd—I feel rather relieved. I had it coming to me, in a way. I am not really very nice to her, am I? Poor little mummie, still crying. I can't have my little mummie crying like that—I'm going over into their room, put my arms around her and say "Will you forgive me, please, forgive me?" She is still sitting on the bed and looks up to me completely stunned. "I—forgive you?" she whispered. I am nodding. I really mean it. I want her to forgive me, not exactly for this afternoon—there is nothing to forgive—but altogether. Just say it's all right. "Say it, please!"

"Yes, I do, I forgive you." Illo stands by as if he were in the zoo watching strange animals. He doesn't understand. But then—neither do I. I only know I had to ask her and she had to say yes. Now she's said it, I am going back to my room to sleep.

Just before I'm dropping off, I feel I've done the right thing, although it is her fault. What is? Buying my short skirt, of course, she knew they don't like them over here . . .

eight

FLYING home to-day. I don't mind. London is all right and it's not so hot. I'm always pretending I like the heat, but it really gives me a headache. And the sun is not good for my skin. Illo says I should not mind, white skin is special. I'll meet my friends and perhaps I can stay with Lilia till the school starts again. I once met her mother, she is like a real—no, I mean an ordinary mother. She's got three children and goes shopping a lot and they have a washing machine. They do their washing always on the same day, Lilia told me. Always on Mondays. Not like some people I know who leave the bathtub full of soapy water and just fling some dirty stuff in any old day and leave it there so that I can't have a bath . . .

Clinic to-day. "You are looking well," says the receptionist at the desk. "Where have you been?" I tell her and she says: "I'd like to go there—how marvellous, did you enjoy it?" I go into raptures

over the sun, the food and the heat and all the
while I am looking at a letter addressed to "Dr.
Magnus Thomas Brockhuus." Didn't know he had
another name in the middle. I'd like to know who
it's from and what's in it.

"I'll call you when he's ready . . ."

This waiting room really gets me. It's nicely done
up, they've really tried. Tried too hard, that's what
I don't like. Goldfish swimming in a beautiful tank
with air bubbles and a thermometer, pictures,
"good" modern pictures, soft armchairs, magazines,
it's not a hotel, it's a . . . no, I won't say the word,
they say it's old-fashioned, and then where would
that leave me; I'd be a so-and-so myself . . . sure
enough there's Bruno in his corner. Still at it. How
often can he do it in one day? Jane thinks it can't
"come to anything"—whatever that means. Still,
he's enjoying himself, grinning all over.

I know that boy over there. He hasn't said a
single word for months. He is very pale and so thin.
He never eats, I think.

Oh, there is a new one, I never saw her before.
She is pretty. And look at her sandals . . .
"Where'd you get them?" I am sitting down next to
her, pointing at her feet.

"I made them." Then she looks at me and says,
"Would you like a pair, it only takes me three
days." Oh I would! "You needn't pay—I do it for
the fun of it."

"Thank you very much, I'd love to have a pair."

She measures my foot and then asks what colour. Black, I'd like a pair of black shiny ones. "Like your hair," the girl says. "They'll be ready in three days."

"You have got a lot of s's in your name," I say to Brocky by way of greeting him. There is the picture with the red squiggles, the black squares and the big yellow blob in the centre. It's not so bad really if one looks at it properly. Maybe one can find some meaning in it after all. The yellow colour has a golden sheen to it, quite soft like a veiled light. There is a new vase next to the telephone on the little table, filled with purple flowers. It's quite safe, I won't touch it. I'm not a child any more.

"A lot of s's?" Brocky repeats, sounding puzzled. Suddenly he understands: "Oh you saw the letter." He smiles at me. "Good to see you back."

He looks truly pleased. Then he sits back in his chair and waits. The old routine. Oh, not this time, Dr. Magnus, Doctor Thomas, Tommy, Tom-Tom. Not this time. None of your "really?" and "why?" and what did *you* think? I'm fed up, do you hear, FED UP! with the whole works. If you want to know something, you'll have to ask. I'm nearly fourteen, you can't play around with me . . .

"Have you been on holiday, Doctor Brockhuus?"

"Yes."

"That's nice. Where?"

"To Spain."

"The Costa Brava?"

"Oh no, I wouldn't . . . we were in Mallorca, up in the mountains."

My, my, that was a long sentence.

"You and your wife?"

"And a friend." More information.

"A man or a woman?"

"Another doctor, we went to school together." He's coming on, isn't he? I'll have some more . . .

"Where did you go to school?"

"In France, in Paris."

"Did you like it?"

"Yes, very much, I enjoyed my schooldays . . ." He suddenly stops. "But you don't really want to know about my schooldays."

"But I do, I do very much. I'd like to compare . . .

"Well, perhaps another time."

"Promise?" I'm smiling like a baby.

"Promise." Got him. He can't break a promise, not as a doctor, he can't. I'll hold him to it . . . a little later. Next time perhaps or the time afterwards. He'll remember.

Then he asks me about Italy. There is quite a lot to say. I wonder where to begin. What does it matter? What am I afraid of? I'll start where I please.

"Mummie tried to kill me." In a conversational tone.

"You must have dreamt it."

"Ask her."

He leans forward to see whether I'm serious. I am. He decides on the spot that I am very serious indeed. He picks up the phone ("Never behind the back of the patient") and dials our home number. I can hear mummie's voice on the other side. "Evalore tells me there has been some trouble while you were in Italy . . ."

Long explanation from mummie.

"No, that's not what I mean, she told me something more important . . ."

Mummie goes on for five minutes without stopping.

"Thank you, thank you very much for being so frank."

I could do a lot of things now. I could smile sadly, or say, "You never believe me" or even "I told you so." But I am sitting quietly and think "your move." Illo says that, when he plays chess with me and I can't make up my mind . . .

"I am sorry," he takes his glasses off and I see his eyes quite clearly, very big and full of sadness. "Perhaps you do not want to talk about it."

"But I do," big tears are rolling down my cheek. I can turn them on like anything; Jane's very jealous of this, she has tried it, but can't do it. "If only we could go for a walk, I can't bring myself to do it in here, here, where you just talked to her." More tears. "I know I shouldn't ask you to take me out again"—I'm getting worked up nicely, I think I'll become an actress—"but I'm so very, very unhappy, nobody likes me, my own mother . . ." A brave attempt to wipe my tears off, then: "Please don't take any notice of me, just forget I asked you . . ."

My head is bowed, arms crossed over my chest, tears dropping on my red skirt . . . it should melt a stone . . . it does.

I feel very grown up all of a sudden. I think it all started in Naples, when mummie had a go at me. Like shock treatment, or at least what I imagine it might be. Only I received the shock knowing what was happening. Bruno said he never feels a thing, a bit dazed afterwards, but it soon clears up.

We are soon sitting in the car and he turns round to me very politely: "Shall we go to the same spot as last time?

"Oh yes, I'd like that. Please."

We sit in silence for a while, looking at the trees and the people passing. It's a lovely feeling being cut off from everybody in our little box. Like a private room. I'd like to put my head on his shoulder again, like last time. I'd like to touch his hands. The more I look at him the better I like him. Why doesn't he look at me? I want him to look at me. Illo always does. He says you can't make contact with people if you don't see their eyes. I have the most peculiar feeling all over my body. As if—as if I were terribly hot and there was a pool and I just had to jump in, I'd die if I didn't . . . Suddenly I am gripping his hand and burying my face in it. His lovely cool hand. It's quite soft inside, like the skin of a fruit. Kissing it very gently, every part of it. I've never done a thing like that . . . he doesn't withdraw his hand, he doesn't say anything. I don't care, I don't care, my face is burning, don't take it away, it's all I want, it's all I ever wanted, my lips are open, gliding all over his hand, it drives me mad this hand, my teeth are closing over it . . . he cries out . . .

There are blue marks on his skin in a half circle at the edge of the hand. I really think I'm mad. Why did I want to hurt him? He must be very angry with me. But—but he's smiling. His eyes are closed and he's smiling. I don't get it. Why does he smile. He looks as if he'd just had a lovely present and closes his eyes so that people don't see how much he likes it. It makes me feel very uncomfortable. My own craziness is completely gone.

Neither of us says anything. But I know. I know something has happened which is so important that one can't talk about it. I also know that I will tell nobody—I'll work it out by myself.

He doesn't say anything either. At least not about—that. He looks at me now, the same way he does at the Clinic, he says, "About Italy. . ."

I am quite happy to talk. In fact, I'm spilling it out as fast as I can. Going on for at least ten minutes.

"The chairlift—you didn't mention that."

"That was marvellous, I enjoyed that best of all. Like a bird."

"Your mother . . . did she enjoy it?"

"Mummie loved it. Said she was sorry she never had the guts to do it before. When we were in Switzerland she couldn't bring herself to go up and she'd been regretting it ever since."

He is prompting me and I'm taking the cues. That's good, that's how it should be. I am quite relaxed now.

When we are back at the Clinic I can't help asking: "When do I see you?" Perhaps he won't want me back after what happened.

"Day after to-morrow, six o'clock as usual of course."

Of course. I was silly to think—

"You are so quiet, Evalore," mummie says at home. "Are you feeling all right?"

Yes, I am all right. But something has changed. I don't know what, but it's all different. Even my pink bedspread and my glass animals on the shelf look different. My school satchel lies forlornly on the table, as if it did not belong to me any more. I must ask mummie to change the wallpaper with the frieze on top. That's for small children, so they've got something to look at. Each wall shows a different fairy tale. I used to like them very much when I was young. I'm sitting on my bed, I can't read, I don't want the radio, I keep seeing this smiling face with his eyes closed and the marks of my teeth in a half circle. I am hurting my own hand so much that tears, real hot tears are streaming from my eyes. Oh, that's better, much better.

nine

LILIA has asked me to stay with her till school starts. Mummie says it's fine as long as I keep going to the Clinic. She packs a little case, tells me to ring her every day and Illo drives me over to Lilia's house. What a place! Three—3!—bathrooms and each in a different colour. I've got one to myself next to my room upstairs.

I've got a lovely bouncy bed and a bowl with sweets on my nighttable and a television just for myself. There is a knock at the door. A maid comes in dressed in black and white, like on the stage. I didn't imagine people really had them nowadays. Did I want anything and dinner was at 7. I ought to wash my hands for a change. Perhaps I should brush my hair? The dining room is downstairs and the whole family is there waiting for me. I've never seen Lilia's daddy before. He's nice. But—he can't compare with Illo. He is just an ordinary daddy, a family daddy. The children, two little boys, look very clean for children. But then they've got this washing machine. Lilia is not as boisterous as she is at school. A little subdued.

Everything goes like clockwork. When the first course is finished the maid scuttles in with clean plates. Then she hovers around waiting to see whether anybody wants seconds. Not much talk going on. Illo and mummie talk at meals. Sometimes we all three talk together at the same time. The telephone keeps ringing and mummie disappears for ages, the meal seems to stop altogether. Then she comes in with something nobody expected, like an avocado pear or strawberries in winter. I've never seen her cooking, she must do it while I'm at school, or maybe she buys it ready for eating . . . Here we've got big plates standing on burners like in a Chinese restaurant. When it's finished, Lilia's mum says to the maid: "Coffee for me and Mr. Golodez in the lounge." There is not a single spot on the white tablecloth.

Lilia is showing me the garden. It's more like a park. You can't see the end of it. Flower beds everywhere and a sprinkler on the law. "Do you like it?" asks Lilia. Of course I like it. It's smashing. Except I would not want to live here. It hasn't got any secrets. No, that's not what I mean. No atmosphere, no feeling to it. There is nothing standing around where it shouldn't. To my great surprise, Lilia bursts out: "I hate this place. I can't stand it. I wish we lived in a slum with rats and mice and dirt and people quarrelling and Radio One on all day and drugs and pubs and everything..."

"But it's so beautiful," I say.

"Yes," she sneers. "I know it's beautiful. I hear every day how lucky I am to live here. Surrounded by all that beauty and tidiness. I don't even have to hang my clothes up. And I'm driven to school and back every day. I like buses. I like the underground. I like the street," she wails. "We never talk in the street—I'm not allowed to go out without stockings," she looks enviously at my bare legs, "even in the summer . . ." She throws herself full length on the grass and rolls over and over in her nice pale blue frock. I have to think of Tuddyfoot when she said to me: "We've got a little firecracker here, haven't we . . ." Lilia is more like a stink bomb. I like her all of a sudden. I like "hidden" people. She asks me about mummie and Illo and seems quite interested when I tell her about my nightmares. She has them too, but not so bad. And she does not wake up screaming.

"I wish I could go to a Clinic too; you must see lots of things there . . ." I certainly do. But it doesn't seem right to talk about it to somebody outside. Even if she is my own age. "What have they got in there?"

I honestly can't say. One doesn't go up to a pa-

tient and say: "What are you in here for?" It just
isn't done. Sometimes they tell you—but you don't
ask. Come to think of it. I don't even know what
I've got . . . except the dreams.

The bed is lovely and I've got a switch for the
television right next to it. There is a religious programme on. Don't care for that one little bit. I
switch it off—must ask Doctor Brockhuus what he
thinks of it. Tomorrow night I'll see him, all being
well.

"All being well?" Am I afraid something might
crop up preventing me . . . That's the bloody limit.
Worrying about not seeing old Brocky. What's got
into me? Old Brocky. Doesn't sound right. Mag.
Magnus. No, Thomas, Tommy, that's better, that's
a new name: Tommy. I think I'll call him—ahhh—
so tired, Tommy, I'm so tired . . .

Breakfast in bed on a tray. Hot chocolate and
butter and jam. Two croissants, like abroad. "Shall I
run your bath, Miss Evalore?" I'm so taken aback I
forgot to answer the maid. She said "Miss."

The bath is as big as a pool with steps leading
down to it and golden rings for the towels. Miss
Evalore is taking her bath. With a handful of bath-
salts thrown in to make it smell good. And a big
spongy cushion at the back to put your head on. I
wouldn't mind having that back in the flat. Maybe I
can pinch the cushion and say I've bought it . . .

I wonder why I'm late. I'm usually on the dot. Then I don't have a bath. At least not the first three days. Must ask mummie or—Tommy. Tommy—Tom—Tom. He'll know, he's a doctor. I will then. I'll ask him to-night. Right to his face I'll say . . .

The pretty girl who makes sandals is sitting in the waiting room. We are both watching the fish in the tanks. She is having her "Do" at the same time as myself. "Hallo, Evalore," she calls out as soon as I come in. I didn't tell her my name. "I'm Loretta—" her name starts where mine finishes. "Your sandals are ready, I've got them with me." She brings out a parcel wrapped in tissue paper. "Let me try them on you—see if they fit." Shiny black leather, just what I wanted. She slips them on my feet and they fit nicely. She buckles them up and tickles my toes. "What nice feet you have, all slim and curvy."

I must say something. "They are beautiful, they really are, thank you very much." It's not enough, I feel, so I say: "Would you like to go to a Wimpy afterwards—when do you finish?"

"Forty-five minutes once I've started." We arrange to meet. She is really pleased. I'm keeping the new sandals on and stuff the old ones in my bag.

"Evalore—Doctor is waiting for you."

I knock at the door. I don't have to do that! I know he is expecting me. Standing by the door I don't quite know what to say.

"Sit down," he says. That infuriates me . . . Sit down. Like an order. I won't be bossed around. Least of all by him.

"I'm late," with a loud clear voice, "I'm two days late with my period.

"Has this happened before?" It doesn't seem to put him out at all.

"No, never, it's the first time." I let a few seconds go by. Then: "It must be all that excitement." Stop. Wait.

"Yes?" There he goes.

"Yes, yes, yes, is that all you can say? Or did they teach you this at the College. Or maybe the books told you. Can't you talk properly? Why do you follow the rules? Can't you make your own? I would think that an old man like you" (right!—he winced) "would be clever enough to find his own way . . . to deal with a patient. But no! You haven't got enough imagination . . . Stick to the book and you'll be all right. No risk. Tidy, neat. That's all *you* know." He looks at me, really does, I've got his attention a hundred per cent . . . Something drives me on, as if I were a woman nagging her husband. "I'm in a mess, I know. I *like* to be in a mess, do you know *that*? I feel lovely, in a real turmoil. I haven't become like . . . like a fossil. I do what I *feel* like doing. Do you? Do you? Did you ever do what you wanted? Without looking at a book first?" I'm off. Can't stop myself, not for a thousand pounds.

"I tell you what you are," I'm standing right in front of him, "you are a coward! A bloody bloody coward!" I'm laughing. Laughing aloud. The room begins to spin and I'm spinning with it . . . singing the same words over and over again . . . my doctor is a coward, a feeble little coward . . .

I suddenly find myself lying on the couch. He sits by my side holding my hands. I dare not open my eyes for fear he will let go. I'm beginning to moan as if I were hurt or in a trance as they do in the West Indies . . . *What* did he say?

"I *am* a coward." I distinctly heard him. I go on moaning and flinging my head about with my eyes closed. He is still holding my hands and now he begins to stroke them. "Quite still," he says, "quite still, it'll pass, it will all pass."

I have my eyes open now, but I'm holding on to his hands for dear life. One look at his face tells me that I mustn't push on. Push on? Where? Where do I want to go? With *him*?

I'm in the proper place all right. I need treatment. I need my head seen to. Bad dreams, my *cul*. Bad wakenings that's what I've got. I'm cracked, round the what's it . . . What do I want? What— do I *want*???

"I don't know what I want," I say to Tommy, very quietly.

"You are finding out." He means it. "To-morrow then."

"Tomorrow?"

"No, no, the day after."

I've made a fool of myself, I'm sure of that. Still, I am quite pleased. He said "to-morrow" by accident, of course. But he said it.

ten

LORETTA is sitting downstairs in the waiting room. She is sitting in one of those deep armchairs which are supposed to make the place look welcoming. She stares at the fish in the lit-up tank. Little air-bubbles drift to the surface unceasingly. The tank gets cleaned once a week. New sand is put in while the fish wait around in a basin, feeling lost and bumping against the plastic walls all the time. Loretta jumps up from her chair as I am coming in. We are going up the road to the nearest Wimpy. She is a little taller than myself, very slim and blonde. Wearing jeans, those lovely sandals very much like mine and a jumper. Funny, she is older and she has less . . . She must be at least fifteen. Maybe more.

Lorette orders as if she's used to it. I never know what to say. And whether I should take a special tone like Illo, so that everybody seems to *want* to do what he says.

"How long?" Lorette asks.

"About half a year."

"Like to talk about it?"

"Well—it's quite simple really. I hate school and sometimes I just don't go . . ."

It *is* simple. One ought not to force people into anything . . . it's bad for them. I don't let them force me. I do what I like and I shall always do just that. The other day I could not face the idea of being cooped up all those hours in that old grey building. I didn't do anything special, I just went for a walk in the sun. Had a cup of tea, bought some sandwiches and fruit and went on the Heath. Flat out on the grass, crossed my arms with my hands for a cushion . . . Lovely, lovely, I could stay like that for hours, watching the sky, doing nothing, nothing at all, and be really happy. I typed out a sick note for Tuddy and signed it with mummie's name. It's not difficult—I tried to copy it, of course, but it wouldn't work, it looked too much like a child's writing. So I simply took some of Illo's dark blue copy paper, put mummie's real signature on top and my letter underneath. Then drew her name with a sharpened matchstick. Easy. Worked like a charm.

Did that for quite a while before they caught on . . . Should have seen mummie. Carrying on as if I'd robbed a bank. Nobody is losing anything by it . . . "End up in jail," she said. Rubbish—my own mother's signature. I think she was too ashamed to tell the headmistress. She made me promise never

to do it again. Illo was wonderful—as always.
"You've got caught," he said, "you'll have to think
of something else," and he winked at me as if it was
a huge joke. It was! It's not like pinching things, it's
just a white lie . . . stupid to get so worked up. I
had to think of something else though.

I went to school for a couple of weeks every day
like a good girl. I even did a bit of homework and
mummie and Illo said to each other "See—I told
you so." They are wrong—they don't know me at
all.

It happened next day at school in the second
period. I started crying just when we did *savoir* and
connaître with Mademoiselle Jourdan.

"What ees the matter, Evalaure?" she asked.
"Don't you feel well?" I shook my head—more
tears. She took me down to the rest room herself
and gave me a couple of Disprins. Never took
them, they are still in my skirt pocket. She made
me lie down and put a rug over me. Nice woman,
but a bit daft. She should have noticed—but then
I'm so good at pretending. I began to look as if I
was really sick. I put a hand on my tummy, tears
pouring down like a waterfall and made her understand it was my period hurting me . . . She became
all womanly and sent me home in a taxi. She explained it to the headmistress who asked mummie
to keep me in bed with a hot water bottle. Didn't
like that very much. But anything is better than
school.

I can't tell Loretta all that—she wouldn't be interested anyway. Then there was that day when I felt I couldn't bear it another minute and just by way of making a change I tore our register up and flushed it down the loo. Tuddyfoot became very nervous, made us open all our desks and went through every one for half an hour. "It can't just disappear," she kept moaning over and over again. Sent me down into the office, to see whether it was there. Took her another half an hour to get a new one going. I do what I can.

There is not that much one *can* do. I often look out of the window and my mind becomes blank—I don't hear what goes on in the class any more, it falls away, it's like waves crashing on the beach, always the same droning noise and in the end it disappears altogether—I just float around in a sort of cotton wool world and nothing matters—then the bell goes and brings me back and I start hating it like a prison, feel I must break out.

Oh, there was the day when I started singing in the middle of maths. Why do they teach us French songs if we are not supposed to sing them? "*Allons enfants de la patrie . . .*" I sang and it sounded so—so wild that the whole class joined in and we banged the desks with our shoes and kept on singing till the headmistress came in and asked who started it.

That's the only time mummie was really nice. When the headmistress, Miss Pringle, rang her she said I have been trying too hard at home catching up with all the schoolwork—and she'd see to it that it wouldn't happen again. If one misbehaves because one has worked too much, that's all right. Pringle came up again and said "Let's forget all about it."

I think they only decided to send me to the Clinic after I had thrown the school meal out of the window. It was a perfectly reasonable thing to do. We have a canteen and the stuff they dish up there—a tramp would turn his nose up, it smells like cat's dirt and very much looks like it. I hardly touch it—if I can avoid it and if my pocket money is not all spent. The others loathe it too. Only they are too meek, they are so afraid all the time what the teachers will say, and will their parents be told.

I like my parents to be told. I want them to know it's their fault for sending me to a school which is so ghastly I can't stand it—I don't want to work there. Why should I work in such a place just to please them? So that mummie is free all day— it's not fair, she does as she pleases, if she doesn't feel like working nobody forces *her*. She lies in bed at all hours and Illo says, "Don't exert yourself, you look tired." Nobody notices what I look like—so on that day, when they slapped some ghastly hash on the plates, it smelt really vile and the smoke curling up over the plate made me feel quite sick, I went to the window, opened it wide for everybody to see and said: "Watch this!" and sent the plate flying into the courtyard.

The other girls screamed with pleasure—that's all they needed. They all rushed to the window and threw their food down too—why do they always need me to start something really good? It made a famous mess down there . . . potatoes and meat and vegetables in a big ugly heap with all the broken crockery; gosh, I wish I had done it before— makes me feel marvellous. The teachers couldn't do a thing, it all happened so quickly. We were sent up to the class and mummie had to come to school. I told Loretta all this in a sort of telegram style.

"Who is your doctor?" Loretta asked.

"Dr. Brockhuus."

"Like him?"

"Hm. Soso."

"Any good?" I can't answer that. I don't know whether he is a good doctor. "And you?"

"Three months. Dr. Liebermann and he stinks."

"Is he that bad?"

"Oh he is bad too, but he stinks like a skunk."

"Couldn't he wash?"

"Maybe he doesn't like soap. Or he can't bear the sight of himself in the bath. Skinny old runt."

We have a Coke each and some crisps.

"Where do you go to school, Loretta?"

"School?" She throws her head back and yells: "School?" Everybody is looking. "I don't go to any (then she said it, but I won't) school. I am working in a boutique. They sell everything, my sandals too, and I get commission on every pair."

My mouth is open. I don't know what to say. And I thought she was a child, like me, well not a child, but young . . . She is sixteen and doesn't live with her parents. She lives in a furnished room all by herself. And she gets money every week-end. She earns her own living. That is terrific. I tell her so and she is very pleased.

"I don't earn much in the shop, but the sandals sell well. I get by."

I think I have never admired anything or anybody that much. But—why the Clinic? If she can keep herself, if she doesn't have quarrels at home—what's wrong with her. Drugs? No, she's not the type. She looks damned healthy. Rosy cheeks, a lovely skin and her eyes are bright and clear. She *is* pretty. I wish I had the courage to ask. Better not, it might spoil things. Usually I don't "like" girls. I've got friends, but I'm not fond of them. I could get fond of her though. She is different. Perhaps she'll tell me of her own accord . . . what she's got . . .

eleven

BACK at school. They've washed the sickly green walls and doors but they look worse than ever. We've even got a brand new blackboard with a special tray for the chalk and a new chair for the teacher. It has a leather seat hammered down with yellow nails. That is about the only pleasant looking thing in the place. The windows have been cleaned. They made an effort—that's obvious. But it is as hideous and prisonlike as before. Just cleaner. Some of the girls have also been abroad. But none had quite as much excitement as myself. I seem to attract it, or maybe I produce it myself. People either let themselves go with me, or I with them. Maybe my "chemicals" upset them . . . I'll ask Tommy to-night. He ought to know about these things. I also wanted to ask him whether he believed in Religion.

There is Loretta in the waiting room all by herself. I tell her again how pleased I am with the sandals and she kneels down to see how they look.

"They suit you," she says and again she is tickling my toes. Then she starts to stroke my legs, saying how smooth they are. It's quite pleasant, her hands run up and down both legs and she puts her head on my knees. Girls don't usually do that to each other, but I don't mind. In fact I rather like it. It's like having a warm furry cat rubbing against you. I stroke her blonde hair—very soft and fine, child's hair. I'm almost sorry when I get called through the loudspeaker to go up. I'm bound to meet her again anyway at my next session. I look at her over my shoulder, close one eye and say: "Same time, same place . . ."

I am—exhilarated. I know what it means. It means: "gladdened, cheerful, lively, joyful, hilarious, playful and excited." Looked it up for my last essay. I am all that. I'm breezing into the room: "Good evening, Tommy."

He looks up. Frowns. Doesn't quite know how to take it. From a patient. But he gets a grip on himself right away. That's what I like. People who can control themselves, who don't give anything away.

"Good evening, Evalore."

"I've got a new girl friend."

"Oh—who?"

"Loretta, she's in the Clinic."

"Loretta Falconer?"

"Oh is that her name. I never asked her."

"Since when?" That cracked down like a whip.

"Oh, a few days."

"How do you like her?"

"I think she's quite the prettiest girl I've ever seen."

No reaction. I have to lay it on a bit more.

"She is intelligent too and independent, living all by herself and earning all that money. I wish I were like her . . ."

"Do you know what she is in treatment for?"

Doctor Brockhuus! You are breaking the medical code—one never asks personal questions about others. Especially one does not discuss patients with other patients. I was going to make some silly remark, like "a little bird told me . . ." but no. Ever since my "shock treatment" in Naples I've become quite clever. And after our little encounter a few minutes ago in the waiting room I don't need to know much more. I'm not a baby. Not that I mind. But he seems to . . .

"I don't know, of course. And I would never ask—naturally. But when we know each other a little better, she might tell me."

"Has she ever . . ."

"Yes?" That's me. Me saying in that tone *yes*?

"Did she ever show anything . . . anything that disturbed you?"

"Disturb me? What do you mean?"

He doesn't pursue this line at all. But his

knuckles are white, because he clenches his fists so hard.

"Do you believe in God, Tommy?"

"I don't know."

"You don't know? But you *must* know whether it's yes or no."

"Sometimes I do and sometimes I don't. It all depends on my . . ."

"Chemicals?"

"Yes! It does—how do you know?"

"I've thought about it," I say modestly. Then, quite seriously: "Please talk about it, as if I were grown up."

He gets up from his chair, paces up and down a couple of times, then looks out of the window into the setting sun. He is very tall, very slim, silhouetted against the window, and I notice the first time what he is wearing. It looks old, that suit, but very expensive. I'm sure he doesn't know *what* he's wearing, it's just a cover for him. That's nice, not like George who is always preening himself like a peacock, wearing a different shirt every day. I hate boys who "dress" like girls, with everything matching. Tommy turns around, takes his glasses off and starts talking. He does not look at me, but this time it does not disturb me. He starts talking, really seriously, but not solemn, he doesn't preach, he just thinks aloud. He thinks for me—because I asked him to: "God—that's a big word. I don't really know what it means. I just want to understand why we are here, or rather to find out why I am here. When I'm seeing other people's minds at work it helps me to get over my own limitations . . ." he stops, asking me with his eyes whether I follow.

I do. I can follow him completely. I'm nodding just once. I want him to go on. Nobody has ever talked to me like that.

"I never found anything in a book I could accept. If there was anything, anything really valid, the whole world would know and nobody would be guessing any longer. There are lots of people who say they've found something, but it always is just their own 'point of view'." He stops again. Then surprisingly: "I wish I could slip out of my skin . . ." This time he stops for good. Brushes his words away like a cobweb.

I'm quick, I'm saying it before he has time . . . "You are not wasting my session, it's marvellous, it . . . makes me feel right. I love to hear you talk like that."

"Right. Back to work."

We proceed as usual. Illo, mummie, school, what I thought of Lilia's family, a lot of old rubbish. I want to "get" at him before I leave. Anything to— to what? He said it, didn't he, to slip out of his skin. I was well on the way with Loretta—I'll take that up: "I don't mind staying a little longer. Loretta will wait, she told me."

"Wait—where?"

"Downstairs of course. She's being cooked at the same time as me."

Not even a smile. I'm the cat, I'm the cat, catch you, catch you . . .

"I like your tie, Tommy. Did you buy it yourself?"

"Where will you go?"

"Oh I don't know. We might go for a walk, or I'll take her up to the house, or maybe I'll have a look at her room . . ."

"I wouldn't do that," like a shot.

"But I've never seen it, there is no harm in seeing somebody's room?"

"No—of course not."

"Then why wouldn't you do it?"

Pause. A very long pause. He looks at his watch. "So sorry, but we've got to finish for to-day." Hickory dickory dock, the mouse ran up the . . . he didn't exactly run, but he got stuck. And I've just eaten a great big saucer full of cream.

I'm still licking my lips when I arrive home. Illo is not home yet. Mummie is typing away. "Tea's ready on the table." Throws her head round for a minute, looks at me and says: "What have you been up to?" and goes back to her story. That's typical. Her beastly stories are all she cares about. They pile up on her little desk and the bigger the pile the more pleased she gets. Pats them, saying "good, good, you *are* coming on." Am I coming on

too, mumsy? Am I? I shall try some of her makeup
. . . she won't like that. She's got a lovely golden
stick with mascara, a sticky liquid with little black
bits in. Hm—not bad, my eyes do look much bigger. Just as I am doing the lower lashes she turns
round and pounces on me. "I told you not to touch
it, leave it alone—at once. Buy your own, what do
you have your pocket money for? Anyway, you are
far too young for that sort of thing."

Mumsy darling, I'm not too young. And I *am* up
to lots of things . . . There's Illo coming home with
a wad of newspapers under his arm: "Did you hear
the news?"

"What news?" says mummie.

"THE News, the latest news . . ."

Mummie yawns. "No—why, is there something
special?"

"Oh only a couple of wars, a change in the Cabi-
net and—"

"All crooks, killers and self-seekers, I'm writing
my own casebook, thank you!"

"Why casebook?"

"Well, if I did in private what these people do in
public . . ."

"Oh you are hopeless—you ostrich! You *must*
know what's going on, how can you live like that?
Haven't you seen what it all leads to if people don't
act, act in time? Do I have to remind you . . .?"

Mummie whirls round furiously. "That's just it, I
have seen it. So have millions of others . . . a fat

lot of good . . . I am not qualified, do you hear?
Why don't you do something about it in your paper, why don't you organise people . . . your ideas'
(she faces Illo, who is retreating a little as if she
was—yes, that's what she is—a small dangerous
snake, she looks like one too, all coiled up ready to
strike, her small eyes glittering) "your 'ideas' have
killed and tortured and hurt more people than an
army of criminals. Ideas, ideals, that's what everybody dies for, that's what wars are all about . . .
somebody has an IDEA and the blood starts flowing—and an ostrich is a lovely animal." She grips a
bundle of papers and waves it about under Illo's
nose—"Here are my feathers!" She throws the lot
at his head . . . I thought he would be angry and
upset. Not a bit. He kisses her. How can he? She is
stupid, really, stupid and superficial, *she* is self-
centred, not caring what happens to the world.

They could have asked me what I'm thinking—
but they don't seem to notice me at all. I wonder
what Tommy thinks about when he is not in the
Clinic. Is he interested in politics . . . I'll ask him.

twelve

I like the looks of him to-day. He has taken his jacket off and his tie. No, he doesn't wear braces. Good. A pair of old trousers and a brown leather belt with a buckle. A dark blue shirt. He looks a bit tired though. Maybe his wife has been upsetting him. Maybe she is as stupid as mummie. I don't know anything about him. Before he can say anything I'm going to do some questioning . . .

"Tommy . . ."

"Why do you prefer this name?"

"It sounds nicer." (He can't object to this—it's a *feeling*!) "Tommy, what do you do when you're not working?"

"Reading, concerts, people . . ."

"Do you—do you ever think of your patients after the work?"

"Often, yes, sometimes one can't help it."

He doesn't seem to mind at all my questioning him. Maybe he is quite glad he doesn't have to sit there like a dummy, repeating "Yes" and "Go on" and "Well" . . . I'll certainly make the most of it.

"Do you come here every day?"

"Yes."

"Morning and afternoon?"

"Sometimes I stay all evening."

"Doesn't your wife get lonely?"

"I suppose she does." Now—now . . .

"Don't you mind? Don't you love her?"

No answer. If he did, if he were crazy about her he would say something. He hasn't. I won't get a chance like that again . . .

"Is she beautiful?"

"She was very beautiful."

Ah—did you hear that?—was, WAS! That's all I need to know, no, not all, I can go further, after all, I must have some fun being a patient, I can say what I like, I am *only* a patient . . .

"Do you make love to her every night?"

Is he going to throw me out? Have I gone too far, I shouldn't have said that . . .

"No." He answered me, he answered my question. Does he mean no altogether or not every night and do people make it every night? I feel like a boxer who has won the first round. Won't insist now . . . I'll skip over it like he does, I've learnt a lot from him.

"Are all your patients children and young people?"

"I get all age groups."

"Do you like older people better? They have so much more to say."

"Not necessarily." I wish I could go on questioning him—well, who's going to stop me, I'd like to know.

"Doesn't it bore you to tears, hearing the same sort of *quatsch* day after day?"

"*Quatsch?*"

"Oh you know, nonsense, drivel, absolute rubbish, one of mummie's words."

"But it's very good for them to bring it all out in the open."

"Is it good for you?"

He suddenly seems to wake up. Smiles. "You little devil," he says, "you certainly know when to strike." If he had said that I'm the most beautiful girl in the world it wouldn't have pleased me half as much. You little devil, he said. That makes me very happy. That's personal. That's very intimate. I'll dream about that before going to sleep. I'll grow two horns just to please him. I'd love to please him . . .

"Evalore, tell me, does your mother speak English to you most of the time?"

"Nearly always. She writes in English too. Says she can't write in German at all, it's blocked."

"Why do you think she says that?"

"Because it's true. She never writes letters in German. She reads German books though. I've watched her. She races through the pages like anything, can't get to the end quickly enough. I've seen her looking at the last page long before she gets there—like a child. There is something odd about her altogether. Sometimes I know things she doesn't —I'm sure other mothers would know—it is as if she has skipped or forgotten a whole part of her life. And now she wants to make up for it. She is really crazy about books. Goodness knows what she hopes to find. Always looking. Always searching, as if she'd missed something and thinks she will find it in a book. Sometimes she breaks it off in the middle, says it disgusts her and plunges right away into a new one. I asked her once and she said it's *thought* she's looking for. Not thoughts—thought. Can't you think for yourself, I asked her. She said, "Now I do, but I haven't had time before—I was so busy keeping alive." That's not very clever is it? Everyone keeps alive. And there was always Illo looking after her. I think she just wants to show off, to make me think that she is different . . ."

"And do you think she is?"

"Oh, she fusses and nags at me like all the other mums. 'Take your coat' and 'Look at your hair' and that sort of nonsense. But she looks different—as if there was something going on all the time I don't know about, nobody knows about it but herself. I don't like her at all when she is like that."

"Like what?"

"As if she were on the track . . . like a hunter, that's it, she follows a track, she's got something on her mind she won't talk about . . . to anybody. After all I'm her daughter, she doesn't have to have secrets from me. I once asked her straight out and I thought she would just push it aside. But she said, 'I can't talk, it'll melt.' Made me try to forget it immediately, by saying, 'Oh, I'm talking rubbish.' But she wasn't you know. I don't like her hugging things."

"Do you like her at all?"

"When I don't see her, when I come here . . ."

"Here?"

"Yes, here. When Illo isn't talking to her all the time, when I have you all to myself . . ."

"Me?"

"Bceause you listen properly. Oh I know it's your job, but it's nice to choose a job where you listen to other people . . ."

He sits in his armchair, looking at me very quietly, very attentively, following every word I say. I would like to see his scar again, I would like to touch it, to . . . without thinking I'm rushing over to his chair, fling myself on his lap and kiss his lips. For one second he holds me so tightly that I can't breathe. His arms are round me, his heart beats madly and I want to die right now, just die in his arms . . .

Then he throws me off, goes to the window, opens it wide and doesn't say a word. I remember what happened in the car. It's not the same now. He sat still in the car— "I'll get you if it's the last thing I do," I'm sure that's how women think, "the last thing I do——" That was round two . . . to me.

I'm slipping quietly out of the room and down the stairs. I know Loretta is waiting for me, but I can't stand the thought. I've got to be by myself. I want to hug myself and keep it all inside . . . mustn't lose any of it. Walking home all the way. Straight into my room; close the door quickly and sit down in a corner by the bed. Putting my head on my arms, so nothing can escape. The feeling is still there, his arms around me. I'm burning.

thirteen

SCHOOL seems even sillier than usual to-day. Stupid girls. All that talk about "boys." I've got a man. Well, I haven't exactly got him, and what is there to get anyway—but I can think about him. *I* don't belong there at all—more grown up. Here comes Tuddyfoot with her row of beads. Two rows to-day. Oh, she can go and jump in the lake. I'll give her a piece of my mind if she . . . "Girls"—that voice, I could strangle her—"girls, we want to see a bit of action to-day. One page right away on 'How the world appears to me'." The old cow. I'll tell her how the world appears to me. And why not? I'll make it so clear that she'll burst . . . What's the matter with me? Why am I writing a delicate essay on my lined paper? I wanted to line up all the four letter words I know and shock the life out of her. Doesn't work. I'm being lyrical, using long words and never want to finish. It's so interesting to describe everything, I could go on forever . . . Old

Boots studies my essays and says sweetly: "I always knew you could do it, Evalore, that's very neat . . ." I'm not even listening. All I can think is "to-morrow."

When I arrive at the Clinic I'm making straight for the waiting room hoping to find Loretta to apo-logize for not waiting for her the other day. But the receptionist stops me. "I'm afraid you'll have to wait quite a bit. You're in the Group now. About half an hour. Tried to get you at home, but your mother said you would come straight from school. Dr. Brockhuus's group. In the Basement."

I'm so stunned that I can only nod, go past and collapse on the first chair. The bastard. The bastard. Why does he do that to me? You know jolly well why he does it. Because he can't do any-thing else. Suppose somebody had come in . . . had seen me sitting there. He'd never get another job as long as he lives. I can see that. But he should have *told* me. He himself. He should have had the cour-age to say . . . to say what? "Evalore, I'm mad about you . . ."? And is he? Or he could have writ-ten. No, that's even worse. So what could he have done? Stick me in the bloody Group, where he can keep me on but will never be alone with me. Right. I don't give up that easily. I won't give up at all. I'll find a way . . . I'll make him—I'm suddenly aware of Loretta watching me curiously. She must have been there all the time. I had completely forgotten.

She comes over and rolls my hair around her fingers. "I missed you yesterday." Ah! Loretta—just what the doctor . . . lovely, lovely, just what I need. "I'm so sorry, Loretta," rolling her name about, "it wasn't my fault, and it was the day before, wasn't it? But I'll make up for it, you'll see."

"They've both transferred us to the Group," Loretta says, "it'll be fun together." You bet.

We are walking down the stairs to the basement. Normally I would feel uneasy, I've never been in a group session before. But now I can't wait to get in. I'm putting my arm firmly round Loretta's waist— I'm sure we look good together, her hair short and blond, mine dark and long—and march her like that into the room. It's quite large and pleasant. Canvas chairs like in a film studio, black and white tiles on the floor, two big rubber plants against a large plate glass window looking out into a wild garden. Sometimes I see patients taking a walk there. I'd like to do that too. Must ask about it. If it were not for the bell right under the doctor's chair . . . *He* is there. I'm not letting go of Loretta and ask him very politely where we should sit. It doesn't really matter where one sits. There are lots of empty seats. About a dozen patients. Bruno is there and Maria and the pale boy who never eats. A couple of others I've seen around in the waiting room or on the stairs. "We'd like to sit together, Doctor Brockhuus. It's the first time for both of us—"

"I understand," Tommy says, not looking at me. "Sit where you like."

I *am* going to sit where I like. I like it right opposite him with Loretta by my side. I'm letting my hair trail over the arm of the chair, hoping she'll pick up a strand sooner or later. Nobody says anything for some time. Then a fat man starts speaking in a high squeaky voice: "I don't like the telephone." Stops. But the others want to know why he doesn't.

"It's not reliable," he goes on, "you never know what happens."

Maria: "But you do know what happens, you hear the person talking at the other end."

The fat man gets up, advances on Maria and shouts at her: "Of course I can hear who is talking at the other end. It's what I don't hear that bothers me. People are listening in, to every single solitary word I'm saying. And they never say anything. But I know they are there. I can tell!" He shouts more and more. "There is a little clicking noise and I know they are 'on.' You can read it every day in the papers. Telephones are bugged, bugged, bugged. . ."

Just when I thought things were going to get lively, the fat man retreats and sits down quietly. He does not speak at all for the rest of the session.

"What did you feel just now, Maria, when Clive"—Clive! he doesn't look like a Clive—"came up to you?"

That was Bruno. He looks much better. And his—I mean, he is properly dressed.

"I was afraid," she speaks very well; I've never heard her voice before, although I know what she looks like without clothes. "I was afraid, but not very much, because I knew you were going to help me."

There was nothing much to be said, it seemed so obvious. The whole thing doesn't get going. Somebody speaks—then there is a long silence. It's boring. Nothing happens. Why doesn't Tommy do something about it? It's his group. Loretta is bored too and starts playing with my hair.

Richard—the pale boy—becomes interested. "Evalore," he says, "that girl is playing with your hair. Why?" I'm looking up at Loretta, as if I had never seen her before.

"Is she?" Then: "Oh yes, you're right. Why shouldn't she? Don't you like my hair?"

Richard says that he likes it very much, but he still doesn't see why she plays with it.

I can feel Tommy across the room as if we were attached by a live wire . . . I am taking my time. "Well—perhaps she likes it too. It gives her a nice feeling. Like fur. And it's good to touch other people. It makes you feel less lonely. I don't mind her stroking it. It's friendly. Some people stroke animals. I wouldn't like that. I don't like dogs. They are always sniffing and snorting." Now I'm laughing outright. "And they can't stroke you, can they?" I am very pleased with the way things are going. Because everybody is waking up and Tommy holds himself stiff and upright, sitting on his hands on either side of the knees.

And nobody knows. Nobody except him and me. And he can't do anything about it either. Unless one becomes violent. Then he'd interfere, I think. But I won't become violent. I don't have to. It's much better this way. "You see," I'm going on softly, "I don't know Loretta very well. But this is her way of showing that she likes me . . ." Richard comes over to us, sits on the chair next to mine and just gapes. The group's attention is concentrated on the three of us, or rather on Loretta's hand twirling my hair around. She is not stupid, that girl. She knows something is happening, she's playing along, obscurely feeling that I want her on my side. She runs her fingers through, closes her eyes and says simply: "That makes me happy."

"You see," I say to Richard, "it makes her happy. Now you don't want me to stop that, do you?"

That makes him very angry. "I do want you to stop it. It's not natural, two girls . . ."

My eyes become very big. "Not natural? What do you mean?"

The chorus: "Yes—what do you mean?" They jump at it of course. You don't get a free show every day. We are waiting for poor Richard to get himself sorted out. He can't. He becomes more and more agitated. "It ought not to be two girls, it ought to be a boy and a girl, who—who . . ." He doesn't know how to finish his sentences. I'll do it for him: "who like each other?" He is nodding: "Yes that's what I want to say: a boy and a girl who like each other, that's clean . . ."

Loretta: "What's clean about that? It's messy, it's disgusting, babies all over the place—ugh!" She means it of course, she does not say this just to please me.

Everybody cuts in, there is a general shouting and discussing and getting steamed up. Tommy is watching whether it gets out of hand. But they all calm down and the session finishes without incident. As we are filing out I'm smiling right into his eyes without saying a single word. I've read somewhere that one must have the strength "not to pick up the phone." I won't. Let him pick it up.

I'm not a child any more. I know what I'm doing. Now I've got something to smile about. Like mummie. I've got a secret. I won't tell Illo. Serves him right. He should have taken more notice of me. Now it's me who doesn't take any notice of him. He'll see, he'll see . . .

I'm walking home again, although it's quite late and dark. It is beautiful to walk by oneself in the quiet streets wrapped up in the night. People will think: who is this girl walking alone? Where does she come from, where does she go? Is she going to meet her lover? It's strange—when you feel so full of secret life yourself how everything around you seems to share in it. Even the street lamps look different. It's starting to rain and the lights flicker on the wet pavement. Now and then a car passes. But the town goes slowly out of action—I can hear my own steps clearly. I could walk on forever in the silent streets.

fourteen

TUDDYFOOT is doing the register this morning. Everybody is there except Lilia. "Lilia? Lilia? Lilia Golodez?"

No Lilia. "Is she ill? Does anybody know?"

"Yes, I do." Jane says that in such a voice that Tuddy looks up.

"Well then?"

Jane bends her head slowly so her brown hair touches the desk, lowers her eyes and generally gives the impression that Lilia has made away with the crown jewels. "I don't know—I can't really . . ." She starts mumbling something about a letter.

"Speak up girl, speak up. What did the letter say?"

Jane appears to wrestle with her conscience. Should she—should she not? "I've got the letter, only she asked me not to let anybody know . . ." Whatever is in this letter, Lilia wants to broadcast it. That's why she sent it to Jane.

"Jane, it is your duty to hand this letter over to me. You may cause great harm if you don't."

The letter is under her French Grammar. "She trusts me," says Jane tearfully, "I can't hand it over. But I can read it out . . ."

Tuddyfoot settles in her chair and Jane proceeds to read. Boots wants to stop her but she is afraid of missing one word of this incredible message. You would think the Holy Ghost is amongst us. Not a murmur, you can hardly hear them breathing . . . and we are always told we can't concentrate. We take it all in, every single syllable. I remember in a brief flash how she was rolling on the grass in her pale blue dress dreaming of rats and mice and dirt . . . Well she's got it now, every bit as she wanted it.

Got herself picked up by a "bloke" in a discotheque and vanished into the jungle round the Portobello Road. Jane is reading the letter aloud. First she is a little shy, but then she warms up, it's so fascinating: "It's the filthiest place I've ever seen with no running water and one loo for fifty tenants, we have to queue up . . ." Jane reads out the Gospel and we hardly dare breathe for fear of missing a single word. Tuddy stands in a corner by the door. I'm surprised she doesn't interfere. We all expect her to leap forward and make a grab at the letter. But then grown-ups never behave the way you think they will.

Jane's voice is quite steady now: ". . . wish you

could see it all—it's dreamy. Wallpaper hangs in
bits and pieces so you can see the bricks behind. No
wardrobe or anything—just a chair and a rickety
old table with a red-shade nightlamp. We hardly
ever get out of bed . . ."—Jane actually blushed
when she said "bed"—"except when Jack pops
round the corner to get some food and a bottle of
beer. We drink from the mug with the toothbrush
and spread the paper out on the dirty sheets. Those
sheets! I think they never change them. They are
black.

"Just as well . . . bugs are dropping from the
ceiling and Jack squashes them with a beer bottle.
What a fabulous mess! Jack's all right. He says I
have the most beautiful—well, he thinks I've got a
lovely figure and it makes him happy to think I've
never been with anybody before. He sure teaches
me things I have not learnt at school. He's very
good at it . . . quite gentle. But—but I know it
won't last. It can't."

Surely Boots will dash out any minute to alarm
the army and the air force. No. She stands still,
watching Jane a little sadly. Doesn't even interfere
when Lilia gets on to Jack and what he looks like.
She can't like him all that much, she is so—objec-
tive. It's disappointing in a way. As if she'd opened
a present expecting a big marvellous surprise and
found a couple of hankies—from Woolworth.

"Put the letter away," says Tuddy, "back to

work." Nobody objects. We can't concentrate of course. The same picture is in our mind. Lilia on that filthy bed with the bugs dropping down and Jack with his strong hairy legs. She's written a text book. No more snooping about in libraries. She's said it all. Now we know. Even little Enid knows—who is never allowed to go out by herself. We've teased the life out of her, because she does not know what a man looks like. Is that what it's all about? All the whispering and giggling and boasting? We all knew about the organs and tubes and things. That was in a book. Not much different from triangles and cubes. But she has seen it all and done it. That should satisfy us completely. Lilia writes well, very lively. She's out to shock, that's true, but one feels she describes it quite correctly. She must have had a great time spelling it all out. Why do I feel so empty then . . . so let down? As if the fireworks hadn't gone off. I had expected a sort of . . . explosion or something terrific like an earthquake and all we got was fun and games. We went home discussing Lilia's letter, going over the different bits and wondering how long it will be before they find her and will her parents let her come back to school or will she be sent away to a boarding school. The discussion is a bit listless. We finish up by talking about Tuddy and how she forgot to give us our homework. It suddenly hits me. I understand. Lilia knows it all, all the words and what they really mean except the one which matters more than everything else. She's left it out.

Love.

All the mothers know and the telephones start humming. Yes, I know it's dangerous. I know there are illnesses. I know you can be beaten up and all the rest of it. Mummie gives me a lecture. I wish she wouldn't bother . . . she really makes me mad. Doesn't she see that she doesn't *have* to tell me? That's what I mean: she is stupid. Does not notice things. And what about her then, what is she doing? And has she never been with anybody else but Illo? For all I know she's had more men in her . . . yes, inside her, than I've had hot dinners. She won't tell me that, will she? Maybe she even now—" For God's sake, mummie, leave me alone, I *know*!" But she won't give up. Keeps droning on about all the unspeakable things that can happen to a girl. Rape. Yes. Murder—yes. She's told me a thousand times. No lifts. Never enter a house if you don't know the people. She really gets on my nerves. What's she dyeing her hair for? And those eyes and, *look*, she has now taken to plucking her eyebrows. Since when? It's ridiculous. I really hate the sight of her. If she were not so small, I would hate her even more. But you can't hate such a small frail person as much as a big one. There is so little of her. But she certainly makes the most of what she's got. It sometimes makes me want to have yellow skin like

her. Gold seems to go with it, looks good that
bracelet. Hallo? I haven't seen that before either.

"Is that a new bracelet?"

"Yes."

I'd like to ask her how long she's had it and was
it very expensive. But that one word shuts me up.
Or perhaps she doesn't want to talk about it with
me . . . it might be a present. But if Illo gave it to
her she could have told me. If he hadn't, if somebody else gave it to her she wouldn't wear it round
the house. She is not that stupid. "Can I see what
your bracelet looks like on me?"

"No." Just like that. She's never done it before.
Always lets me try her things on . . . I want to tell
Illo about it. It's nasty not to let me try. I wouldn't
break it, her precious bracelet. I'm very careful.
But I decide that I won't tell Illo—it's too babyish.

Illo is marvellous of course. When he hears
about Lilia he just laughs aloud. "Mrs. Golodez
would give her right arm for it," he says.

"Illo!" says mummie reproachfully. Doesn't impress him.

"She would too—just for one day." Tops—as always. No sermons from him. "As for Lilia," he goes
on, "it couldn't matter less. She is without possibilities." Now what does that mean? Mummie asks
him. Again they are talking as if I were not present.
They never run out of topics, these two, after all
those years. "Not like Evalore. You can't tell with
her. She changes from day to day. There are a

thousand roads open to her—that's the beauty of
it—a thousand roads and she wants to go them all."
I really love him. It sounds beautiful, like a fairy
tale. A thousand roads like the Arabian Nights . . .
I see myself standing at the crossroads radiating out
from the centre like a star and I am walking on all
of them, sometimes coming back to the beginning
and sometimes jumping from one to the other half
way. But what is half way and who will tell me
which one is the right one? Will Illo help me—do I
want him to help me? I hear Tommy's voice. "Do
you? Do you?" My heart starts aching all of a sudden as badly as it did that time in the car when
Tommy smiled at me. I've got to see him, to talk to
him. I must tell him all that. He said I could ring
up the Clinic if there was something urgent.

This is urgent. I must talk to him, I must hear
his voice.

"Don't pick up that phone, you clod! You stupid
nit, do you want to ruin everything? What would
you say, what? Can I come and sit on your lap?
Moron. Think, think! Don't you dare touch that
phone. Don't you spoil your 'possibilities.' Eat an
apple, turn on television, have a row with mummie—anything . . ."

"Evalore, how do you feel about the Chinese
Restaurant?" says Illo.

"All three?"

"Of course all three. Did you want me to
starve?"

Not him, no. "But mummie looks so tired . . ."

"There is nothing like sweet and sour pork to revive a tired mummie . . ." and he quickly bundles us into the car.

I am so grateful.

fifteen

I'LL meet Loretta in the Park before our next session. I owe it to her. I can't make excuses all the time and she was very good in the Group. Never asked me anything. It's nice to walk with a girl who is so interested in you. It's attractive . . . I like her to take my arm and we could both walk together in step, if only she wouldn't try to touch me more than I want her to. But it's not important, it doesn't do any harm. And I need her. I do. Better play along with her. She does look nice with her fair hair and a green silk scarf. We are sitting on the grass, emptying a box of chocolates as fast as we can. She always brings me something to eat, or to drink, and she wants to pay for me when we go somewhere together. She says it's natural for her to pay as she is so much older.

I accept that. I pretend, of course. I know she wants to bribe me. That is a very pleasant thought. Somebody likes you so much that you get presents for just being there. She must want me badly, because she hasn't got much money. That makes it even better. I like to be wanted. We've found a little secluded corner behind a hedge by the lake. Not many people come here. We can sunbathe or read or talk. All three together sometimes. Loretta puts her head on my knees and starts stroking my legs. I'm always stopping her when she goes up higher than I want her to.

It's hard to stop her to-day. "Please," she says, "please, just once—I'll do anything you like." Her face is flushed and her eyes are closed. Anything I like.

You are a little devil, you know exactly when to strike . . . I do Tommy, I do. "Anything?"

"Whatever you say."

"Then talk about it—to-night."

She does not understand. "Talk about this? About you and . . .?"

"That's what I said. You don't have to say—that you've done it. Just that you want to."

"In front of all those people and the—" She gets up like a shot. "You, you—it's *him* you want to know!"

"Yes, you're quite right. I want him to know. Take your choice." I am a thousand years old. She begins to stroke me again and I say quite firmly: "If you don't talk I'll never go out with you ever." She prefers me to go out with her. And it's not bad— just once. I wouldn't want it to go on though . . .

Not for too long. Can't say I dislike it altogether. Makes my skin tingle. She strokes me all over and starts kissing my legs. Starts rubbing her soft blond hair up and down. Ah, that's nice, I like *that* . . . "Do it again, Loretta . . ." She goes crazy and rubs her head against me, burying her soft fair hair in my lap. I push her away suddenly. I think she wanted to . . . "Somebody coming?"

There is nobody in sight, but she stops immediately. Slowly opens her eyes as if coming out of a dream. Doesn't seem to know where she is. "Somebody coming? Where?" There was nobody of course, but I couldn't let her go on. It felt like— like a little dog. It's got to stop. She takes both my hands, puts them on her hot face and murmurs my name over and over again. Nobody has ever done that before. "Evalore, Evalore . . ." as if it was some kind of magic. I can't follow her—it's too intense, perhaps that's how people behave when they are in love. It's terribly late by now and we hurry out of the park.

We had to run all the way, we nearly missed the beginning. Just made it. Everybody is there. What a lot of glum faces. Tommy too—looks rotten, tired and old. I'll wake you up, sweetheart. (First time I called him that, even to myself.) Got news for you. Or rather Loretta has. I meant what I said. No talk—no outings. No chocolate boxes and no hedges by the lake.

Clive is not there. I heard that he got worse and

had to go "in." It's a smaller Group to-day. That suits me fine. It will come off better. I'm just in the right mood for a real blow-up. Start by telling them all about Lilia. But I don't make too much of it— just preparing the ground. I'll go into politics, I think. Better than acting. It's more powerful and it's real.

"So what," says Maria, "she goes off with a chap. What's so special about that?" Quite right. Anybody can do *that*. I don't even look at Loretta. We both know that is her cue.

"It's not so special," she begins in her low pleasant voice. As she talks very rarely everybody listens. She takes a deep breath. "I want something quite different. I don't like men." Good girl, good girl. She must like me an awful lot.

"Oh," Maria again, "what do you like then— horses?" Nobody laughs.

"No, I like girls." I do admire her guts. That was not easy.

"All girls?" Richard asks curiously.

"No—just one."

I don't take part in the talk at all. I don't need to, because after she said that they all talk together. "Who—who, do we know her, what do you do with her . . ." They get very excited.

Tommy's voice: "Will you please keep calm. You'll upset Loretta." That's a good one. She *is* upset all the time about me, about ME . . . It's me it's all about, don't you notice anything? They haven't, because they keep pressing her to say who it is she likes.

She doesn't say. She says she can't bring herself to say it. They respect that. If you can't make yourself say something, it's no good insisting. "But you can tell us what you do, can't you?" Loretta agrees. She could if she tried. They sit back like in the front row of the stalls.

Not a word from Tommy. His hands are clasped together tightly. Again I feel the connection between us as strongly as if we were tied together like Siamese twins. I even know his thoughts: "How can the Group forget that little scene with Richard the other day, when he said . . . it's not natural, it ought to be a boy and a girl!" But Tommy (I'm starting my private little dialogue with him which really never stops). Tommy, they are not involved, that's why they have forgotten. You are not so clever for a grown-up man. I know that. When you don't care you forget.

I have not forgotten anything, I remember every single solitary word you ever said. Every gesture. Even before I look at you I know what mood you are in . . . how far I can go. I know you best when you don't say anything at all, then I can hear your thoughts. I wish you would write to me. Then I would know you by what you leave out. That's not schoolgirl's stuff. It's perfectly true. "Outing: Dr. Brockhuus—Evalore." It's hung up in my mind like a picture—each letter clearly defined. I don't have to look at your face. I'm watching your hands so tightly clasped together, the knuckles standing out like small rocks, all white.

Loretta does her stuff really well. X certificate and some more. She goes on in her low voice as if she had to wrestle with every word. She doesn't give them too much—I love to understand people and why they do what—quite good at it by now. But then I've had months and months with Tommy, trying to get things sorted out. That helps a lot. I know for instance that she gives them only bits and pieces, because she must hold some things in reserve, so that I will see her again and again. That's as it should be. It's—civilised. That's the word. She wants something from me, I want something from her. We swop. The group has something to think and talk about. Tommy ought to be grateful. It's a good lively session. He's got something to think about too. His wife can't give him that! What does she give him, what is she like? I'd love to know. *Was* beautiful. Is she all shrivelled up? Is she small like mummie or perhaps very big and strong and good to him when he's tired? Ask him! And why not? I can do as I please, that's what the sessions are for. Get it all out of your system and make the others join in . . . We are all patients, they are not supposed to shut us up . . . the doctors. The doctor.

Loretta has stopped talking. She pretends to be thoroughly mixed up and seems to regret she's said so much. Her chin almost touches her chest—she's so embarrassed, I don't think. We make a fine pair, we ought to do an act together. That makes me giggle. It *is* funny—that's what she *wants*.

"Why do you giggle, Evalore?" That's the German girl, Gretl. She is terribly serious. She has only been here a little while; nobody knows much about her. She wears glasses and can't stop looking at the numbers on coins. Not the big numbers, but the year they came out first—1960 or 70, this kind of thing. She can bear some years but others tie her up in knots. When she sees the wrong numbers she starts screaming and throws the coins on the floor. She gets pills—those bloody pills. I've had them ages, three times a day. Didn't make a scrap of difference. On the contrary, the dreams got worse. Now I have one in the morning and one at night. They are supposed to calm me down. They don't—I tell you they don't.

I'm not calm—I don't want to be. What's the good of being calm? I want to kick up a fuss and get into a whirl and swivel about, all hot and steamy and dangerous, like Vesuvius, make them watch me, worry about me day and night . . . I'm giggling some more and then I say: "I just tried to imagine . . . what Loretta said . . ." They have all been doing it, of course. But I said it. I'm honest. That shuts them up. I've noticed that people don't know what to say if you really tell the truth. I think most people prefer a couple of stupid lies. It be-

comes so bad that they don't know any more themselves when they are lying. They become so boring
then. I don't mean little things—where you have
been and what you did. That's practical. But what
you feel. It's marvellous to say exactly what you
feel, it's a fresh bubbling sensation, like a brook,
cold and clean and rushing along not knowing
what's going to happen at the next bend . . .

"Do you want to marry, Gretl?" She doesn't
know what to say—see what I mean? Her pimples
light up like beacons and she must feel very hot because her glasses become steamy. "I don't know
. . ." she manages to bring out.

"I want to marry." I'm warming up. "I'd like to
marry a man who is just like me, only the opposite."

"He can't be both," Gretl answers.

"He's got to be, or I won't marry him." My heart
is beating just a little quicker when I go on: "Are
you married, Doctor Brockhuus?"

I don't give a damn whether you are meant to
question your doctor, but I think you are. After all,
he is a member of the Group and we are very modern here in our open Clinic. If he shuts me up . . .
but he doesn't of course. He knows me too well.

Richard says you can't question your doctor.
Other people think I can. Tommy says very kindly:
of course you can question your doctor and I am
married.

That, sweetheart, was a mistake. You should

have said, but I told you that already. Or perhaps, but you know I am married, we have talked about it in the private sessions.

As I said: I know you by what you don't say. You want to pretend it did not happen. Well you are trying too hard.

"A long time?"

"About forty years." Second mistake, dearest. You know that I know. "Forty years," I am overawed, "that's an awful long time—you must be very old. How old are you?"

"I'm fifty-nine."

It sounds as old as the hills. But I don't care. He can be ninety-nine and I wouldn't mind. Years are nothing. I would like to go on, but something warns me to stop it for now. I felt it in his voice, a little clipped when he said fifty-nine. I let it go, but the battle is on. I'm in a good position, I think. I don't misbehave, so he can't make me leave the Group. His heart is in his work, so he won't leave. And I know he enjoys a good fight. And—he enjoys me. I know that. Whatever you say, whatever you don't say . . . I know.

But somebody else starts misbehaving. Gretl of all people. "Fifty-nine!!" She is shouting this number over and over again. "Fifty-nine, fifty-nine, take it away, I can't stand this number . . ." Her voice rises all the time till it's such a piercing scream it bounces back from the walls. She is spinning around wildly, knocking chairs over and one of the big rubber plants, screaming this number at Tommy. Why doesn't he do something? He ought to know . . . he's in charge. How strange—he is nodding and saying to Gretl: "You are right, Gretl, perfectly right. It *is* a dreadful number, it is the last possible number, after that .´. ." The patients don't know what to make of it. I do. Gretl is calm all of a sudden and grins at him: "That's right. It's the worst of all—too many loops. The five and the nine . . . very bad." She goes back to her chair. That's one thing settled for her: 59 is the worst of all. The doctor said so.

sixteen

MUMMIE has got her golden dress on, the one with all the buttons down the front and large sleeves. Either something special is going to happen or has already, or she wouldn't have put that dress on. Although I know nobody else who would put on such a dress in daytime I see that it suits her and her surroundings. How different her room looks when Illo isn't there, slightly oriental with its low seats and an enormous Chinese vase on the floor. There are coloured tiles on the wall which she brought back from Fez: a lovely greeny blue.

She gets up from her writing desk, puts a hood over the machine and looks at herself in the three-sided mirror on top of her dressing table. She grins at her own image, dips a forefinger into one of her little make-up pots, slaps some green on her eyelids and surrounds the eyes with fine black lines. It really does make them look bigger.

"They have taken it." "It" is her latest story, the

one she said was better than all the rest put together. A big continental review is illustrating it
and translating it into several languages, French,
German, Italian and Spanish. The review comes out
in four languages. She is radiant: "Let's celebrate,
let's do something marvellous! Shall we go out—or
would you rather I bought something nice for you,
would you like a dress, or a bag, or maybe a new
pair of shoes?"

"Mummie, I'd like some shoes—but I'd also like
you to talk to me."

"What about?"

"You—when you were little. Your school—anything."

For once she understands. We are buying a
lovely pair of shoes with big clumpy heels and then
we are going to a place where they have cream
cakes as large as a house and all the fruity drinks
for her. It's more interesting with Loretta, because
there is always a lot going on between us, tension is
the word I think, but this is nice too and I really do
want to know about her. She is my mother, after
all, and I ought to know something about her life. I
have two cakes and a coffee—I watched her, but
she did not object—and she has a big glass with
fruit bits swimming on top. There is music from a
record-player, but it's so soft, it could be drifting in
from anywhere.

It's pleasant to sit here with my mother.
Mother—that's the first time in years I think of the

word—not "mummie" or "she" or some nasty swearword. Perhaps she is not as bad as I think. After all it *is* very nice of her to take me out because she is happy. And she let me choose the shoes I liked best and did not say they wouldn't stand up to bad weather. Thought she would object to the colour. Red as a letter box—doesn't really go with any of my things, but it's such a lovely colour. "They will show up your pretty feet," she said. That's just what I thought. None of your "it's not right for your age" . . . I wanted them and she bought them.

And she is not jealous of my cream cakes either. If only she were not my mother—that's not very clever. Then she wouldn't have bought my shoes and would not want to take me out to help her enjoy herself.

She ordered my things first and saw that everything was all right. Sort of . . . protective. I feel soft and light inside . . . nothing bad can happen to me. When I was very small and sat on her lap when I'd fallen down and hurt myself, she was stroking the hurt and it did not seem to matter . . . That's how I feel.

"Please start: Once upon a time . . ." I must be barmy. I'm not a baby. But she takes it seriously. Her lips open a little, she looks quite young and pretty and starts talking: "Once upon a time there was a pale little girl living in a big house. There was a high wall round the house so nothing would disturb her life. There were people to teach her and people to cook and sew for her and all her family was always around her with lots of children to play with. When she was ill doctors came to the house and her grandmother sat by her bedside and told her stories which were so funny that she hoped she would be ill a little longer.

"She never thought about being happy or unhappy. There was so much to do and the days passed one after the other so smoothly that she hardly noticed that she was growing up. The same people were around, the children were always together and the girl's parents were kind and clever. They sometimes went on long journeys with her into foreign countries and she learnt lots of languages. But they always came back to their beautiful sheltered house and there was grandmother waiting for them with cakes and flowers and coloured paper bits fluttering from the entrance.

"But as she grew older there were less people coming to the house. The grown-ups talked together in whispers and she heard terrible stories about what happened outside in the world, about death and murder and people disappearing overnight and that there would be a war more horrible than anything they had ever seen. The best thing would be for the children to leave the country and for the grown-ups to stay behind, sell the house and then come and join the children in a foreign country.

"But the other children did not want to leave. So the pale girl set out all by herself . . ."

Mummie suddenly stopped and bit her lips. I don't want it to stop.

"It's like a fairy tale. Please go on, mummie, please."

"It's not a tale, but it's the only way I can tell it or else I will cry and cry . . ." She does not look like a snake at all. She looks sad and fragile and I feel that perhaps I ought not to make her go on. "Where was I," she says, "what did I say?"

"You said the girl went off all by herself."

"Yes . . . She arrived in a foreign land and had no money and did not know anybody except one boy she had known when she lived with her parents in the big house. They were happy that they had each other and got married. There was nothing to eat but they were still happy. The boy studied and the girl learnt how to sing and they thought they were going to have a marvellous life.

"But the war came and they were separated and put in prison."

Mummie stops again. Just when it gets fascinating.

"Let's go home," she says, "I can't control myself." She speaks to me as if I were her age. "I'll tell you the rest, I promise, I want you to know . . ."

I am getting up reluctantly. Because I feel she won't go on at home . . . it's so familiar . . . the everyday surroundings. But she throws her coat on the bed, sits down on the floor and just starts where she left off ten minutes ago. It must have gone on in her mind while we were walking, because she is using almost the same childlike, far-away voice as before:

"The prison was very dark and cold and the people in it were as pale as ghosts. Every now and then the door would open and food was pushed in—always the same food—and then the door would be shut with a bang and a key turned in the lock.

"Sometimes the prisoners were taken away in the night and we heard shots ringing out in the court-yard. We tried to sleep on the hard stone floor but it was too cold, so we all huddled together and sang softly in the dark night because we were too sad to speak.

"After many days the doors opened and we were taken out into the street. The sun was shining and we were free to go where we liked."

I notice that she is saying "we" by now and not "the girl" any more. The nearer she comes to the present time the more she says "I".

"I wandered around in the strange country, meeting lots of people like myself, just out in the sun for the first time and we formed a little band and looked together for food and shelter. We shared everything we had . . . but I did not know . . . I did not know . . ." She can't keep it up any longer. Tears are pouring down her face and she sobs: "Illo—I thought I had lost him, I thought . . ."

I am crying too, it's all so sad and I've never seen mummie like that before. Pity that Illo is just coming home at that moment. Now I'll never hear the end. He takes one look at mummie, sees her crying and says: "Why did you upset her?" That is a nasty thing to say. For once mummie is on my side. "She didn't, Illo, it isn't her fault at all." But it's gone. The feeling I had for a moment is gone. There are no fairy tales for me.

seventeen

I'M getting fond of Loretta. Not in the way she would like me to, although I mind her less and less, perhaps if she wouldn't be so insistent—but the way she behaves in the sessions is really marvellous. I let her do what she wants, well more or less, and she gets it all out, slowly, reluctantly, as if she had to *force* it out, every single word that passed her lips. The group is very disappointed if there is no new "instalment" forthcoming.

She says she is feeling so guilty about it and only when she can tell the group and get rid of it all can she feel easier. I'd like to see the fiend who would prevent her feeling easier. By now there is not an inch of my body which she has not described in loving detail, except one—but she's got to have something in reserve. I've become quite observant all of a sudden. Up to now I never noticed much.

I heard what people were saying all right. But I did not really look at them. Hearing and looking was too much. Tommy makes me do this, of course. While Loretta is speaking I never take my eyes off him—in a guarded way naturally. I don't stare at him. I always thought that his eyes were dark like Illo's. But they are deep grey with little black flecks. White eyebrows—how odd, why white? He's old, that's why . . . But I like them, they make his eyes deeper, oh, I love his eyes, even when he closes them. Then I know what he looks like when he is asleep.

He closes them quite a bit lately. Concentrating . . . I know what you are concentrating on! Me! That's what. Like the rest of those little stinkers . . . No life of their own, not what I call life anyway, chewing over the same bits again and again. It gets so boring.

I don't feel like waiting for Loretta to-day. It's such a beautiful evening. There is still a little light lingering in the sky. I'm slowly going up the road wanting something to happen, really *happen*—a change, a new thing, something big and striking and unexpected. Ah—that's Tommy's car, isn't it? I love his car, it's so like him, a little old but like nobody else's.

Why doesn't he close the windows—Illo always makes sure his are closed—anybody could . . . For God's sake, don't you touch this car! Too late—my warning system doesn't work any more. I'm trying the door. Not locked. Well then, what can you expect? It's an invitation. He might as well put a notice on the windscreen: Come in, it's all yours, make yourself comfortable.

That's the third time I'm sitting here. But I'm alone now. I've got all the time in the world. He is always staying behind to do some work in his room upstairs. There are gloves, a book about the Incas, a road map—nothing much. But it's lovely to sit here, seeing the sky getting darker and imagining him sitting next to me. Heart just missed a beat. He will be—sitting next to me. I am not going to get out of that car. And if I have to wait all night . . . I am not leaving my seat. Something takes over and tells me not to think ahead. Just sit. I can always say I've been with Loretta.

Must have dozed off. It's pitch dark. The car door bangs shut and he sits down behind the wheel. "And where have you popped up from at this time of night?"

I'm wide awake at once. "I am sorry"—stretching my arms and yawning my head off—"I didn't mean to stay, but I was so awfully tired after tonight's session. I thought you wouldn't mind." I just keep talking, anything to prevent him throwing me out on the spot. He does not even try. Detached, but very kind, very understanding. He could take me up to the main road and drop me at the bus stop. No, my darling, you are not going to drop me at the bus stop. My mind's made up. I'm strong, strong, I'll make you do just what I want and just what you want . . . I'll fight for it. He won't resist much, I can feel it. I am speaking quite calmly while my blood is racing in my body a million miles a second: "You are so unkind, having this lovely car and making me go by bus; I'll have to wait ages at this time of night, take me up a little further, then I can walk home."

"I'm not unkind." It sounds like a little boy.

"Well then . . ." I say this very softly, "If you are kind you would take me for a little ride. Just ten minutes. It's such a lovely night, and I won't say a word if you don't want me to, we could go straight ahead, we need not speak—just because it's right and beautiful and the stars are out." I am hypnotising him—I am! I keep on talking in this soft voice not to break the spell: "I am so lonely, I never have any fun, nobody cares about me—but you are different, you are like nobody else in the whole world, you are the most marvellous doctor (on purpose this). Everybody else is conventional, sticks to the rules, but you—you are special . . ."

Does he even hear it? He drives on and on, very fast by now, houses whizzing past, lights, shop windows reflecting for a brief second the flash of the dark speeding car, I am singing inside. Oh God, don't let him stop, keep him at it, on and on, we are racing along, there isn't another car on the road, just fields now, trees and a few lit-up windows . . . Don't stop, my darling, don't break the spell, I'm so happy.

I must have said this aloud because he stops so

abruptly that I'm almost thrown out of my seat and says, "But I do not want to make you happy—at least not this way."

I know better than to answer that. Without moving an inch from my seat I am stretching out my right arm and pull his head down. My lips are open. So are his. I think I'm dying, I think I'll kill him if he stops.

He does not stop, but whilst I'm almost drowning I can feel his hand on my shoulder pushing my dress away and digging his nails in so deeply that I'm screaming with pain. "Stop it, Tommy, stop it!" He doesn't hear. He is now sitting upright and I can just make out his face. He is smiling. Smiling! That same secret smile he had when I hurt his hand the first time he took me out. He digs his nails in deeper and deeper till I almost faint with pain. I can't bear this another second . . . Ah, he's taken his hand away. Why, why? What have I done—I don't understand. Why does he hurt me this way? I thought he liked me, you don't hurt people you like. You can be mean to people you like or tease them or even embarrass them, as I do in the group sessions, but you don't hurt them, you don't hurt their bodies . . . We are driving back now and, strangely enough, we are talking, just ordinary talk. The group, school, Illo, even Loretta. Neither of us mentions what happened out there. I don't want to think of it. I'm discovering that there are things one must not think about. Dark, secret things which must not be stirred up. That's a rule. Don't mention it, don't ask him. I don't want to know . . . and it wasn't that bad anyway. I think I imagined he was smiling like a big cat in the jungle while he—no, stop, finished, nothing happened, I had a lovely drive, my shoulder is hurting a little but, but what does that matter? I'm sure he did not do it on purpose. He can't have done. He just got so worked up he did not know any more what he was doing. I'm stupid really. There is nothing to it . . . we'll soon be home. Home—that's a nice word.

"Can you drop me just at the corner of my road, please . . . and thank you for a lovely drive. We must do it again."

I know we won't drive out again and I also know neither of us will ever talk about it. I won't even tell Loretta . . . It's sinking away already, I can feel it disappearing as I'm quickly jumping up the few stairs to the flat.

Mummie and Illo look rather worried. I feel quite sorry for them. "I tried to give you a ring, but the phone didn't seem to work. We all went out together after the group session and just continued talking, it was so interesting, I quite forgot about the time . . ."

They are so relieved that I'm home, they don't ask me anything—off to bed. I like my room. It's so cosy with my furry pink bedcover and the little pink standing lamp by the bed. There's my clock with the mouse on it—it's for children but I keep it just to remind me of when I was small—it's ticking away and makes me feel safe.

That was a truly horrible dream I had. If only I could remember it properly, it's important. I know I was in a big house in a cellar and somebody kept shouting at me to jump out of the window. But there was no window. Not even a door. Dark stony grey walls and no opening anywhere. I was so hungry and thirsty. Very large apples and oranges and bananas appeared on the walls, but when I wanted to get hold of them they became flat like paintings and had no substance . . . "Jump! Jump!" that voice kept on shouting, but he can't have meant it, how can you jump when there is nothing to jump out of? "Now, now—if you don't do it now, you will never . . . never." What was it? What was it I would never do?

I wish I could remember. If I had written it down right away like Tommy told me to. Maybe it will come back later, although dreams hardly ever do.

eighteen

LILIA is back at school. Tuddy pretends that nothing has happened. We all know Lilia's mum has been besieging the headmistress for days. She doesn't look any different now. Same old Lilia in her pale blue beautifully cleaned cotton dress. White shoes and bag and not a bug in sight. She doesn't get any peace from us in between lessons. Maybe we are jealous, maybe we just want to know, to hear her say it, instead of having it read out with Jane's tearful voice. Jane's very quiet lately. While we are hammering away at Lilia she never says anything.

Lilia is right among us answering questions, but not making too much of it. It's like an interview— quite matter of fact.

"Have you seen him again?"

"No, my parents collect me from school every day; I couldn't, even if I wanted to . . ."

"Don't you?"

"No—not really, a week was quite enough."

"Did you really like it?" We badly want to know.

Lilia smiles graciously like a queen to her humble subjects.

"It's all right—if it doesn't go on for too long. Want to see his picture?"

We almost tear it out of her hands. There is this big fat gorilla with a stupid grin and a badly cut suit.

"How old is he? What is he called?"

"Jack. I told you in the letter."

"But his second name?"

"I wouldn't know—I never asked."

She never asked. That floors us. She spent a whole week with him, bedbugs and all, and never asked his name.

"Why didn't you feel like asking him?"

Shrugs her shoulders, doesn't put it on. "I wasn't really keen. He showed me something I very much wanted to know. That's all . . . What's Tuddyfoot's first name?"

Everyboy is very impressed. We never even thought she *had* a first name—you don't think of teachers like that. Perhaps I'll bring the whole topic up to-night at the session. Yes, it will be a lovely topic to throw into the discussion when he—when they least expect it.

Everybody is there. Gretl spits on her glasses to clean them. That's disgusting.

And I don't like the way she dresses. As if her

pimples weren't enough to make you want to run
. . . checked gingham dresses like a school uniform
and black patent leather shoes with spiky heels.

Maria and Richard have become quite pally. She
is very attractive with her clothes on and she does
her lashes well . . .

I really *am* more observant; I notice my surroundings and what people wear. I could describe
every detail of this room with my eyes shut. The
beigy comfortable canvas chairs, the grey carpet on
black and white tiles and the pictures with lots of
greenery and little houses with red roofs. Supposed
to cheer us up . . . I'll cheer them up all right—

"I'd like to ask something I can't understand . . ."

"About Loretta?" They haven't had their ra-
tion—beasts!

"No, it's general." Pause, Why doesn't anybody
say something, why do I have to start, or Loretta?
Why doesn't Tommy say anything? Does he think
of the other night, when—there is nothing to think
about, nothing happened, we had a drive in the
country. Doesn't work. I can still feel the spot on
my shoulder. It burns through my clothes like fire.

"How often do people make love?" I said that
very clearly.

Somebody says "sex maniac" half-heartedly.
That's what we come to talk about. Everybody is
aware of that. We've tried other topics, but it
doesn't take us five minutes and we are back at it.

Some think once a day, some once a week. We can't agree.

I'm kicking Loretta: "Ask him, come on, ask him," out of the corner of my mouth.

"Let's ask Doctor Brockhuus," she says in her low deep voice. "No use quarrelling about something we don't really know . . . How often do you think people do it, Doctor Bruckhuus?"

"It depends on the age and the constitution, maybe also on the surroundings . . ." his voice trails off.

"What is the best age?"

"When one is young, naturally."

"When does it stop?"

"It need not stop at all when you get older."

"But how often—how often in a night?"

"As I said, that depends entirely on the constitution."

"How can you tell—beforehand?" That'll earn her at least one outing in the Park. She's a real pal.

"You can't. People don't know themselves."

I'm kicking Loretta's shins, she shouldn't let him off now.

"Is there an average?"

"I should say twice a week."

"Is that what you do?" She should have a medal, that girl.

"I am not average, I am an old man." He's got her. But he has not got me. I'm not saying anything. With a slow, deliberate, obvious gesture I am putting my right hand on the burning shoulder. Leave it there. He's seen it, I can feel him getting a tight hold on himself. I've told nobody, my hand says, but I won't let you forget it, as if you could.

"I'm keeping a diary." I say this out of the blue, as it were, as if I wanted to change the subject. This time I've scored a direct hit. He closes his eyes for a brief second. The fraction of a second—while lightning struck him.

Gretl and Maria keep a diary too and the session goes on. But the evening belongs to me.

It's quite true that I am keeping a diary. I did not make this up for his benefit. Illo brought me a beautiful folder when he came back from the States. It's a map of the world in all colours, but ancient, like they imagined it back in 1499, with Italian names on it, or perhaps Latin. I write something in my diary every night, except when I'm too tired. I haven't got much of a background—I mean family, aunts and cousins, not like mummie who grew up with lots of people around. That kept her sane, she said, when she went to all those terrible places, that she had such a happy childhood. Then things can't get you down completely.

That's why I'm making up my own background, it's all in the diary. The people I meet and what I think and where I go. I started to make a list of all the books I'm reading. But I can't keep it up. Once I made a little pocket inside the cover, where I put small pieces of material from the dresses I used to wear. That reminds me of all the years past. I'm now thirteen. There is not all that much to remember. It's just this year, these last months . . . things begin to happen suddenly. I don't make them happen, one can't do that.

I wish sometimes I were like Lilia. She hates— and she says she hates. Runs away, comes back, it seems all the same to her. And I can just imagine how Mr. and Mrs. G. carried on when she finally arrived after her Portobello week. I wish I were little again; I could talk to Illo and tell him everything. But I'm too old now. That same evening, when Tommy hurt me so much in the car, I could have talked—when I was really upset. But now I've got to cope with it myself. Did not even put it down clearly in the diary. It's there, of course, but it's hard to say what really happened.

Why is it so important? There must be other things in life, like jobs, or hobbies, or, or what? Mummie says she divides people into two categories. The ones that make her fly to the sky and the ones who make her sink to the bottom of the pool. Does Illo make her fly all the time? Do I? Who makes me fly? Illo, Loretta, not all that much, but a little. Tommy? I've read an article about a Laser beam, a beam that can cut skin and flesh and bones. That's what he does to me, Tommy.

I adore listening to a really outsize row; like to see

them getting at each other. They try to keep it for evenings, "It's not good for children to see their parents fight" (children!)—what nonsense. There is nothing better, it's like a play. I can hear them now, getting warmed up for it. It usually starts with some practical thing they did or did not do and then it becomes general. It's amazing how a little thing going wrong makes them question everything about them, about them being together. They are closing the door carefully, so the floods won't escape, but I can hear every word. I can even open the door when they are really at it—they would not notice if the house fell down.

Illo: "The Shelleys are coming to-night, why aren't you dressed?"

Mummie is flopping around in her Japanese dressing gown. It's a real one, or was, with long butterfly sleeves almost down to the floor, only she's cut the sleeves off because they got caught in her typewriter.

"They are not coming. I've got a headache."

"But you look perfectly well. What happened?"

"Nothing *happened*. I just dis-invited them."

"There is no such word."

"Then I've just made it. I dis- out- uninvited them, couldn't bear the idea, talk talk, talk, a load of rubbish . . ."

"But they are friends!"

"Ha! Haha—ha!"

"I was looking forward—they've made their arrangements, you can't do a thing like this at the last moment."

"I bloody well have."

"Don't use those words—they're for kids."

"Meaning?"

"Those words belong to a certain age group and it's not yours."

I've opened the door just wide enough to see them. Illo is pacing up and down and mummie stands quite still. She is like a little ball of fury or rather like a bomb ready to explode. She has no reason to be upset. Especially as they are Illo's closest friends. And it's quite true what he says. She should not use swearwords; they belong to us, to young people. Illo's lovely almond eyes have lost their soft looks. I love his eyes, they've got large lids, round and silky; I like to stroke his eyes when they are closed. Mummie does not appreciate him at all.

". . . stuff it . . ." Couldn't hear the beginning.

"You have no standards, no principles . . ."

"Principles—what FOR?"

"Something to live by, to hold on to, to use as a yard stick, to . . ."

Mummie still does not move. But her eyes look really dangerous, like little icicles, hard and sparkling. Her voice is very low: "I've managed quite well without them, thank you."

Bother, can't hear, they have moved to the window. I just get snatches: ". . . all those years I was away, how did you manage to . . ." She must have said something really nasty. Because he starts shaking her. She doesn't seem to mind, because she put her hand on his shoulder quite calmly and says in her natural voice:

"But I didn't like *any* of them, you know that."

"Didn't you—didn't you and what about . . ." Can't catch the name.

Mummie opens her little eyes to saucer size and says: "Who's he?"

Illo is stunned: "But you must remember, for years you . . . One can't live like that. You never tell me the truth, I don't know where I am, you can't have forgotten, you said you were asleep and you only woke up when . . ."

"I don't know what you are on about. I'm tired."

"Tired? You? How can you be tired? You do what you like the whole day long, while I'm slogging my guts out for you!"

That's torn it. Now the big scene. Their voices rise and, with the window wide open, they don't care who hears them. I would like to feel they really hate each other. But just when I'm thinking he is going to strangle her or she'll run away for good or at least for a little while, she starts giggling and says his eyes look like big rolling marbles and would he look in the mirror "you big ape" and she calls him something in German which sounds very nice and tender, getting round him in this—this female way I hate. Then they both look into the mirror, he puts

his arm around her saying "so much poison in
such a small pint" and kisses her.

I'm back in my room. I loathe it when he kisses
her, especially after a row . . . when he seems to
like her *more* than before. Nobody kisses me when
I'm nasty—I just get told off. Why aren't people
nice to me? I'm not bad looking really, with my
long dark hair and Illo's eyes, only lighter and my
lashes are longer.

Loretta calls me "sleeping gypsy"—sounds goods
but doesn't count, she *wants* something from me—
she'll say anything. Mummie says everybody goes
by what people look like, but it's not true. That is
terribly superficial, looks are not everything. Or?
When I saw Tommy the first time I remember
thinking quite stupidly: he is far too good looking
. . . for a doctor. Why should a doctor not be good
looking? It's being shut up with him in the room
alone. But that was about six months ago—I was a
child then. But still, I knew right away there was
something special between us.

The way he said "Evalore?" when I came
through the door. And he pulled up a chair for me
as if I was a woman. Now I'm stuck in this idiotic
Group. I've got to do something about this. I'd love
to see him alone. Not in the car though—but in the
Clinic. I'm a woman too, I can get round men just
like mummie. I'll find a way, I've got brains. I
know!! Oh that's marvellous, that's clever. I'll do it
right away. Sitting at my desk—I'll use my new

fountain pen: "Dear Dr. Brockhuus," I'm writing, "I feel so bad about my relationship with Loretta that I would like to talk about it when she is not there.

"I know you are very busy, but it's only this once and won't take long. I've got to get it off my chest, I can't sleep properly" (That'll get him—he's always telling people that sleep is more important than food, and if you don't sleep properly you don't get in touch with your "Self" and you destroy yourself . . .) "and I don't dare tell my parents, because I don't want to get Loretta into trouble. I've nobody to turn to and I'm really very unhappy. You are the only person who would understand and be able to help, I am so alone.

Yours Evalore"

"Dr. Brockhuus will see you the day after to-morrow at 6 pm before the Group meeting." From the Clinic on one of their little white cards. I'm glad—more than glad, I really am happy. He *will* see me. He will also hear me and I am going to make the most of it. I won't get another chance so easily. I'm five minutes early, with my tiny red skirt, the Naples skirt, and a white jumper, as tight as can be, one size too small, on purpose, you can see—I'm a girl. I'm usually looking at the magazines, but can't concentrate now. What do I really want from him? Could it be true that I feel bad about Loretta, now that I begin to like it? No, I don't feel bad at all, but I do want to see him all by myself, I have almost a craving, a real hunger to see him, to hear him talk, just talk to me, not to the others. They don't know him like I do, they don't see him as being so special, so different, they do not feel as if an elastic band pulled and tore at them, until—until, "Evalore, Doctor is ready for you!" I turn the waterworks on just before I open the door. Not too much, I'm not *crying*. I come in with my head bowed. I'm beginning to feel very sorry for myself.

"Sit down, Evalore. Make yourself comfortable." Impersonal, kind.

"I was longing—to talk to you, I can't to anybody else."

"So you said in your letter." I am suddenly lifting my head and a beautiful big single tear runs down my cheek. He can't quite deal with that. He didn't expect this single tear. Maybe a flood, or me bursting into sobs—he would have known what to do. He would have brought out his hanky and said, there there, and that would have been the end of it. Kind doctor, poor little patient in trouble. I don't want that. Just now in the waiting room I did not know *what* I wanted. I do now—I want to sit on his lap. But HE's got to ask me. I want to make him feel so that he can't do anything else.

"Doctor Brockhuus" (didn't expect that either) "Doctor Brockhuus, I feel so guilty when I'm with Loretta." He is going to repeat one single word, I'll bet a pound on that.

"Guilty?" There!

"Yes—mm—very. I used to let her do what she wanted, because it made her so happy and it didn't do me any harm, but now . . ."

Long pause. The doctor waits for his patient to go on. To get it out of his system—her system—so she can feel better and rake up some more muck. Only the doctor starts digging his nails into his hands again, that's not on the programme, I know where he wants to dig his nails in . . . If only he wouldn't look so perfectly marvellous with his pale skin, like silver, as if the moon was shining on him, his dark grey eyes almost black with the effort to remain the kind, understanding, patient doctor.

Patient—that's a laugh. *He* is the patient—he is the one making a great big effort to control himself. The more he tries the better I like it. I feel easy, I feel there is nothing I cannot do if I really put my mind to it. I am wiping the tear away with my little finger and go on: "But now I am almost enjoying it, I am almost waiting for her to start."

"Start what?"

You asked for it, my sweet. "Touching me, kissing me, to stroke me and . . . and . . ." Little Evalore is so confused, she doesn't find the right words. She is so embarrassed, she blushes all over. I remember Illo shaking mummie when they quarrelled. I'd like him to do that to me. He doesn't do that. Instead he is gripping his leather belt with the buckle so tightly I think he'll tear it to bits. Takes a deep breath, lets go of his belt. "Go on!"

"I can't . . ."

"But that's what you came for."

"I know, I will, but I've got to make myself . . ."

All the blood is gone from his face when he says: "If you can't do it to-day, let me know when you are ready, we can't leave you in this state . . . Make the appointment with Mrs. Reynolds. I'm sorry but I have to take the Group now."

He gets up and sees me to the door. I'm popping into the loo opposite, turn the key and do a little war dance. I don't need drums, I don't need flutes, I don't need anything. I've got it, I've got HIM! So sorry he has to take the Group. I bet he's sorry. He'd rather have me. Thank you, God, thank you, for making him do that. My skin tingles, I see myself in the mirror, my head thrown back and my hair lashing out like black feathers.

An appointment with Mrs. Reynolds! That means I'm back, back to the little room, where I'll have him to myself. "We can't leave you in this state." "We"—I like that. He wants to know. Loretta did not leave much to the imagination, but he doesn't know what *I* feel. That's what he wants to know. When mummie has been a real devil she always sings a little song about Rumpelstiltskin: "Oh how good that no one knows" . . . his real name.

It's a dead secret which nobody must discover ever, or else he's in their power. It's a fairy tale. I've seen it in a German book, a little gnome dancing about on one leg in the middle of the wood, big fir trees and mushrooms as large as straw hats, wild flowers everywhere. It was a coloured picture. Deer peeping out from behind the fir trees and a little hare sitting on his hind legs, the gnome turning round and round and singing this little song: "Oh how good that no one knows." No one knows what I'm up to. Loretta thinks I'm getting a kick out of driving him up the wall, she doesn't know that I'm longing for him, as if I wanted to eat and hadn't had food for a whole month. It's a real craving. Can't get enough of him.

Is that what people feel when they are on drugs? Richard told me that the longing is so strong, one can kill and stab and rob—just for one shot. It sort of takes over. You have no will any more. Is he like a drug for me? Is that it? Oh, it does not matter, as long as I can look forward to something terrific . . . I don't mind waiting a little, as long as I have something to wait *for*—and there are always the sessions downstairs. They will be so much better, knowing that there is something else!

"Oh how good that no one . . ." *It is* like a fairy tale, I'll make it into one, with big Gothic print, spidery and strange, and lots of coloured pictures. They will all show a pale man with silver eyebrows and a little girl. No. I'm not little—children can't wait. I can. I can wait a hundred years as long as I get what I want . . . in the end.

nineteen

MRS. Golodez has invited me to go to a show with
Lilia. Thinks I'm a "good influence." Some daft
classical play at the Old Vic. Trust her! Why doesn't
she go with us? Because it'll bore the pants off
her. "Oedipus"—who wants to know? We get
enough of that at the Clinic, thank you very much,
nobody takes *that* seriously any more, especially
after Gretl (she is coming on) said to a new boy
who is crazy about his mother: "Don't feel
so guilty about it, just have a complex." Even the
boy laughed as if she had made a discovery and it
helped him no end! Much better that the patients
help each other than the doctors . . . It's more
natural.

Why does Lilia's mother buy tickets for a play
like that? It's not exactly "suitable" for young girls,
is it? But it's classical and that makes anything
suitable. How stupid. Still, we've got very good
seats and I like the intervals, when you can talk and

watch the people in the audience. The chauffeur drops us at the entrance.

It's not at all what I thought. I imagined lots of stuff on the stage and the actors wearing those white garments, standing rooted to the spot and just reciting their speeches, making grand gestures and shouting away.

But the stage is empty, except for a huge golden dais standing in the middle. And the actors wear modern dress, not proper suits but something made of dark wool which looks as if you could wear it now and not a thousand years ago. Two thousand perhaps. I never know . . . What's that behind me, that odd hissing, buzzing noise, like a thousand wasps?

It's not only behind me, it's all round, it's spun like a net through the whole theatre. I've got to see. But they are everywhere, the actors are dotted all over the place next to the pillars, on the balconies, in the stalls, right up to the roof. They are speaking, but I can't make out the words. I don't need to—don't have to hear what they are saying, but this noise, resounding almost from inside yourself, I've never heard anything like that ever, this noise, this fizzing, rustling insisting hum. I'm sitting in a cocoon, I want it to stop, but I don't—no, it must not stop, I would fall if it did, I would come down with a bang. The golden dais on the stage opens up, a figure appears. I know the story, of course, we've had it over and over again when we did Greek mythology.

But although I do know it, it is not at all the same. It lives, I can feel it living—now. I'm swept into it, as if I were part of the play. That's never happened to me. I thought theatre was something you looked at and listened to. But this: I don't know where I am, I hardly know . . . what I am. It's like a spell. I can't take my eyes off the stage, the droning voices all around me become more and more insistent, they almost make me jump out of myself. When the curtain comes down in the interval I feel as tired as if I'd done lots of very hard work. But I want it to go on, to get at me as before, to sweep me on to the stage, into the golden dais . . .

"What a load of old rubbish," says Lilia, eating chocolates. She squeezes three into her mouth at the same time and a little bit of pink stuff oozes out at one corner. I feel sorry for her. She's seen "life" in the raw, she's had her *experience* and here she sits eating chocolates, when I'm almost bursting with too much feeling. Must have a look at the programme:

"What has four legs at dawn
     two legs at noon
     three legs at dusk?"
it says on the first page.

"It's obvious, isn't it, Lilia?" Not to her it isn't. "But it's man. He crawls on all four legs at first . . .

then it walks on two, and then when people get old, they have to use a stick. That's it, that's their third leg . . ." Now I want to know who wrote it. I think that's the first time ever. I usually never look at the print in a programme, just the pictures of the actors. Seneca. I've heard that name before, no, not in the class. I know I've seen him, I remember his face, very bony, with a short beard, very long modern hair, and a sort of Roman nose. I can't have seen him, he's dead, Roman nose, Roman . . . of course, of course: Naples. In that museum with all the naked statues. His head. That was about the only thing I liked. He looked so clever. He wrote this play all that time ago. I'm reading up all about him, while Lilia goes on eating. He killed himself. Perhaps he was too clever—he knew too much. Perhaps he saw things people are not supposed to know. Or maybe they did not like the way he wrote.

I can slip right out of my skin as soon as the curtain goes up. I'm sitting down here, but at the same time I'm up on the stage, as if I were speaking, or maybe I'm making this strange noise all round, this new noise, but it doesn't seem so new now, it seems I've always known it. I've made it inside myself very often, I've moaned like that when I was unhappy, I've hissed and groaned in my sleep, in my nightmares, but this *is* a nightmare, this is the most terrible nightmare I've ever seen. I think I'm going to drop . . . "Another chocolate, Evalore?" That came just at the right time, I thought I was going to faint, it was too much.

The play goes on and when I think it's over there is a big mob of people streaming on the stage. They are jumping on to it from everywhere—behind me, from the top, from the front row. The whole theatre is swarming with them. Their clothes glitter and they make some sort of modern music, but is it modern? It's very loud and shrill and goes right through me. Now they are doing some mad frenzied dance round a large golden object. It's right in the centre of the stage, looks like a male organ. But they wouldn't dare, would they? Putting something like that for everybody to see . . . in a theatre? But there it is. It's huge and threatening, like a monstrous big tower. It's frightening, it's upsetting. They should not do this, frightening people who just come to be entertained—but why not? Why is it bad to be shaken and upset?

I'm beginning to think it isn't all that bad, because they show us what is true. Love—that's what it is all about. *That's* what I want to talk about, if I'm really honest. That's why I don't mind going to the group sessions, that's what I want from Tommy. That's really what I want from . . . no, no, that is stupid, stupid—I have not ever thought that before, it's that crazy music which makes me think crazy things . . .

That music and the glitter and the noise and all these dancers swirling around make me dizzy. I want to be like that, I want to join them up there and dance and scream and swirl around with them, then I would feel free, wild and free and I could sing and pray and wouldn't want to hide anything, not even my thoughts.

Pray? Why—I have never ever prayed except to say, please give me this or take that away, or make something last . . . I feel a little shiver down my arms, because I think that's what they *are* doing . . . They are beside themselves and they are praying, I'm quite sure. Perhaps there is no other way to pray. But this isn't a church. You could have this free giddy feeling anywhere, if people would give you the right stuff . . . I'm exhausted, I can't think any more, I can't feel any longer, it goes too deep, I'm only thirteen, I'm not supposed to follow the grown-ups, perhaps they make it all up to be special—or I'm not ready for it. That was a very grown-up thought! Lilia is quite happy with the last scene. At last she's got something to giggle about. "The size of it," she says. That's coarse . . . She's missed the point, that's the only thing she will remember. It's all wrong, she's got it all wrong.

Got a new teacher at school. A woman, of course. I'm sure a man would be much better for us, we would listen more. But no, another female for Geography. We are quite used to old Tuddy, but this new one . . . I know we are not going to get along with her. She is strict. Far too much. A little bit is all right, but she overdoes it from the start. We are even afraid to sneeze. She looks at us as if we had broken the ten commandments, if we simply ask whether we can be excused. And this one is married. Mrs. Barge . . . very suitable name. Names are funny things, I don't see why they always fit people. They do—although she is more like a battleship than a barge. I don't envy her children and, anyway, what does she do with them when she comes here? Are they grown up? How old is she? Forty or thirty or what? Square face like a bus and as red. It's not made up red, it's natural. She wouldn't go near a tube of make-up, I think. Her hair is permed; that's ghastly, little grey squiggles all over her head. Bet it feels wiry, don't envy her husband waking up every morning to *that*!

"Sit straight," "Don't talk," "Repeat what I said" . . . for God's sake, this is not a school for soldiers. We've got to stand up when she comes in the class and remain standing while she calls out the names from the register. That's a bit much. I know why she does it—I've heard teachers talk. "You've got to establish yourself right away or else the kids will eat you alive". What nonsense, real *Quatsch*!

Establish! What a horrid word. Means you won't change even if you ought to. We don't like you at all, Mrs. Barge, and I'm not going to remain standing to-day when she does the register. I am not standing up for anybody . . .

"You—you there, in the second row . . ."

"My name is Evalore."

"I don't care if it's Jesus Christ, will you stand up at once."

"I would like to, but I can't."

"And why can't you when everybody else can?"

"I've got a fracture." Haven't the vaguest idea what it is. Sounds OK.

"Oh—have you seen a doctor?"

"Yes, yes," (in a pitiful whimper) "my mother takes me three times a week to the hospital"—I'm not even lying—"and they said I must not stand for the next three months, or it will crack."

She does not insist. Stupid mutton, all curly and stupid. The class has caught on. It's becoming a game, and there's nothing she can do about it. We are not rude, or nasty, or cheeky. We are playing. How do you fight people at play?

Lilia sits down with a bang. This is fun. "The green dress in the front—I haven't given you permission to sit down." Then Lilia said it, it will go down in the school's history . . .

"I must not stand for too long, because of the baby . . ."

Barge doesn't say anything, then, slightly put out: "What baby?"

"I'm only in the third month, but even so I mustn't . . ."

"You are *what*?"

"The third. But I must be careful. May I be excused . . . I will have to be excused more often than before. I hope you don't mind."

That's the stuff heroes are made of. I didn't think she had it in her. There is a terrible uproar, we are forgetting all about the new teacher, when Lilia sails back in we pretend to believe her and nobody cares about the Far East . . .

When the Geography class is over and Mrs. Barge has regained her composure, "No more nonsense to-morrow", we cluster round Lilia admiringly. She dared! We are asking her: "Whatever made you think of that, Lilia?"

She smiles. Looks round with her big blue eyes, is almost beautiful and says: "I hardly ever think of anything else—it's true."

For five minutes nobody says a word. We believe her instantly. You don't invent that tone of voice, calm, cool, and very different from us. She is apart. Right away. She jumps over the fence into a different country. Yes, she will stay on at school another month or so. Then her mother takes her to the country. The gorilla knows and wants to see her. But she doesn't want to see him. She would like twins, one of each. And she is going to keep them. You are not supposed to bring up children when you are thirteen, but she is going to get a nanny. All worked out. After all it would be rather nice—they've got that big house and the garden.

As we leave the school we see her sitting with the headmistress in the office. Lilia is opposite her with

her legs crossed and her face propped up on one elbow . . . a visitor.

"A girl in my class is having a baby," I'm saying
in the Group.

How old is she? Did she want it? What did her
parents say? etc. etc. It is discussed in great detail,
because some people in the group are quite a bit
older than myself, and they want to know. There is
nothing I like better. I tell them all I know and then
I say that I wouldn't want one. Never thought
about it till now, I'm not sure either way. "You
will," says Maria, "later on you will . . ."

I'm turning on her rather angrily. "How do you
know I will? You know nothing of me, how can
you say I shall want one? I don't, I don't!"

"Why not, Evalore?" That was Tommy. Why
does he suddenly interfere?

"They take your freedom away, you have to stay
home all the time and you can't go out and meet
your friends, and all the washing and—and your
figure becomes bad, you have to look after it day
and night, you talk of nothing but babies all the
time and you become boring, so nobody will want
to talk to you but other mothers."

"Is your mother like that?" Tommy again.
What's got into him?

"I'm not a baby, she does not have to stay at
home, she does as she jolly well pleases . . ."

"But when you were small?" This is not a private

dialogue, Doctor. This is a group. Let us get on with it.

"Of course she looked after me then." She was pushing my pram with a silky blue cover, saying my baby is so big, such a big girl, too big for her little pram, I can remember very far back lately—and when I fell and hurt my knee she took her scarf and bandaged it and carried me all the way home.

"But now she does not need to, I can do everything by myself, she does not want to look after me any more, she wants people to look after her, people who—have enough to do as it is, people who work all day, and then she expects him to listen to her every word and what she has written and where she's been . . ."

"My mother never goes out," says Richard.

"Well you're lucky then," I snap back at him. "Mine does. She goes out all the time and never tells me where she goes and when Illo asks her, she's got it all ready. I think she is lying, she does not go where she says she does, but Illo believes her, because he never lies, and he can't understand how anybody else can . . ."

"How do you know she is lying?" Who does Richard think he is?

"I just know. By her voice—she talks very quickly and as if she had it all mapped out beforehand."

"But maybe it's true, why should she be lying?" Richard insists.

"She's got secrets, I know she has, you only have
to look at her . . ." I feel a bit lost. I can't prove
what I'm saying, but I know.

"Why doesn't your mother go out, Richard?"

That is nice of Tommy. He's seen I got stuck and
he wants to help me. He knows when I'm uncomfortable. Loretta doesn't know. Would not care if
she did. She's got one idea on her mind. Full stop.

Richard's mother doesn't go out because she
hates towns. Potters about in her garden all day,
grows her own vegetables and salads and pretends
London is a village. No wonder he went "to town"
and was drawn to the worst places. Isn't there anybody normal in this world? Not here, not in the
Clinic . . . they *wouldn't* be here. It's really the
parents who ought to come, it's all their fault. Why
can't they be like everybody else, like Jane's
mother, who doesn't mind when she comes home,
or Lilia's parents . . . But then Lilia isn't like anybody else either. No, it does not seem to work this
way. In my case it does. Illo is fine, it's mummie
who should be different. Oh, I'm getting a bit fed
up with all this digging and searching.

What are we looking for anyway? I'm not ill. I'll
ask Tommy next time I see him alone and none of
your "what do you think." I don't think, I'll let him
do the thinking for me.

twenty

FULL of beans—I'm just in the mood for a real "Do" with Tommy. You have to be in the mood, like an actor or a composer, then it will go off with a bang. "Good evening, Tommy." He knows my mood right away; he's always one jump ahead of me. I like that very much. It's a challenge, like a race, see who gets there first.

"Good evening, Evalore." He looks great.

Looks *are* everything. He is so—what's the word I'm looking for?—delicate, so sensitive. He couldn't do his job if he weren't. Oh yes, I wanted to ask him.

"Tommy, what am I coming to the Clinic for and please don't put another question to me, I really want to know." He does not answer right away. Looks at me very seriously then opens his hands palms upwards as if to say, that's a tricky thing to be sure about. His eyes—they plunge into me, they go down to the bottom, even if he doesn't know ex-

actly what I'm thinking, but they know me, the real
me. The window is wide open, there is a lovely
smell of trees and flowers. It could be so marvellous, so wonderful, if he weren't a bloody psychiatrist . . .

But if he was an ordinary person like everybody
else, if there were not this distance between us,
maybe he wouldn't seem all that marvellous to me.
I'm beginning to enjoy this distance. It gives me a
bit of space to move around in. "Possibilities" as
Illo would say.

"That's what I'm trying to find out," he says
when I had forgotten all about my question. "Why
do you think you are coming?"

"Because of those dreams and because I'm no
good at school. It worries mummie—much more
than Illo, he doesn't seem so upset, but mummie
. . . she worries herself sick."

"About school?"

"No—not really."

I feel as if a dam were going to burst and I'm
shouting: "The jealous bitch! My own mother—she
can't bear the three of us together, because Illo
doesn't pay any attention to her at all when I'm
around. I'm young, I'm new, I'm interesting"—I
can hear my voice screeching but can't stop—"He
knows all about her little games after all those
years. He must be sick of waking up to the same
face each morning. She can't even be bothered to
take her make-up off, there are little black dots all

over her pillowcase. It's hideous." I'm spitting with fury, it's been kept under for so long. "She isn't even pretty, just tarted up. But he's not taken in by that, oh no, he can see the difference."

"What is the difference?" Tommy asks, quite matter of fact.

"She is old, old and worn out and self-centred . . . never talks of anything but herself and her beastly stories. She bores him stiff. Her tantrums . . . She throws things at him, you know!"

"Carnations or roses?" Tommy asks drily.

"I'm only imitating her." It does not sound very convincing.

"Why would you want to do that?"

I don't like being caught—I'm not answering. But I know he won't let go. My fury is gone and I feel embarrassed. Why would I really want to be like her when I think her so horrid. I can't understand. I've had treatment for so long, I cannot just push things aside. As I'm so involved with Tommy, I never stop to ask myself why they insisted on my coming here in the first place. Other kids are bad at school, and I know lots who dream terrible things.

"Tommy," I'm saying timidly, "I can't answer your question but I know that I'm changing."

He looks up sharply: "How?"

See? I'm not as stupid as some people think. I know how to make him sit up. I will say the truth and nothing but . . . It works better—at the moment. Maybe he'll extend my treatment and cancel the Group. If he feels he's on to something he won't want to interrupt. I am looking at my little golden watch and say "Oh!", because my time is nearly up. I put a lot of regret in this *oh!*, as if I had been prepared to have a good go, but I wouldn't want him to feel it's his fault that I can't go on.

"No call for the next half hour. Can Dr. Lieberman take the Group till I come down." He replaces the receiver with a bang. "How are you changing?"

I am looking to the floor for fear he will see in my eyes how I feel. A prize-fighter. A gladiator who has thrown his net over the enemy. I've seen pictures: head thrown back triumphantly, one foot on the body under the net . . .

"I used to lie all the time, even to myself. Perhaps I lied most of all to myself. I don't now—at least not all the time. Since I've been coming here"—I'm giving him the grateful-patient look—"things begin to look clearer, I feel so much easier in my mind, so much happier." I'm not even putting it on.

"Your mother—why would you want to imitate her?"

"That's hard to say." I'm biting my lip, it's absurd. He's quite right to ask.

"She has her good points," I say reluctantly, "I only notice them when Illo isn't around. When I quarrelled with Jane in front of her the other day she said gently: "You are both right. Jane is right for *her*self and Evalore is also right for *her*self.

Two opposite things can be right at the same time,
like the two tracks of a railway." I liked her for
that. It's clever. Just as one can be happy and unhappy at the same time. Or as the hot sun shines on
the snow and the snow doesn't melt when I'm ski-
ing."

"What were you and Jane quarrelling about?"

"Jane thought you can be in love with two
people at the same time and I said then she is in
love with neither. And another time mummie understood when I said I wish I could rub out all the
awful things at one go. "Living is like making a
drawing without a rubber," mummie said and then
added softly, 'I got it from a book.' That sounded
lovely, like a little girl trying not to show off.

"But then, if she is so clever, why does she let me
get away with everything? She never punishes me
except once when I . . . when I tried to . . . when I
was fiddling with my safety catch on the chair lift.
She nearly choked me. I liked that—in a way. I
had it coming to me. But she never hits me, neither
does Illo. It's stupid!"

"Do you want to be hit?"

"I would prefer it. Yes."

"To what?"

"To those idiotic conversations. What have I
done and why and didn't I see I was acting against
my own good and so forth. I'd rather have a quick
hurt, I mean a real sort of body hurt and be done
with. First she makes me feel as if I were her equal

and then she tells me what to do. It's cheating. I never know where I am. They can't talk me out of things, I'm too young!" I finish, surprising myself: "I want parents, not pals."

"A jealous bitch, who has her good points but is falling down on her motherly duties, because she doesn't give you a good hiding now and then," Tommy sums up smilingly.

That's about it. It does not sound all that convincing, but maybe true things never do. I'm smiling too because I found out such a lot.

"I wonder how I could sum you up," Tommy says to me.

"But don't you know? After all, I've been seeing you for months."

"Sometimes I think I'm sure, then you take a jump and I've lost it." He is perfectly serious. Not trying to evade the question or anything. He likes to be clear about it, but he just is not yet. It's so lovely; I don't feel I have to get at him, or provoke him, just be with him and talk.

"What kind of jump?"

"A jump in time." I don't follow that at all. He goes on: "There sits a little girl with her toes turned in and right before my very eyes she grows and grows and suddenly there is a—"

"Woman?"

He is nodding twice. "Yes, a woman."

I'll go just one step further, I'll *be* a woman.

"A nice one?" He smiles and the whole room

lights up and I'm in a mood, like that day we saw that play, off the ground and in a sort of fever— nothing counts but everything is possible. I'm getting up, moving towards him, watching very closely and, as he sits quite still, I'm sitting down on his knees very gently and put my arms around him, my head on his shoulder.

"We can't—" he says very close to my ear. That's all I need. He said "we." That means he wants to, but doesn't dare. It's taboo. I know what that means. You must not do it or you die or something terrible will happen to you, like floods or fire or typhoon—I'll outwoman all the women . . .

"But I'm not really a woman, it doesn't count, I'm just a little girl who needs—comfort. Hold me, Tommy, hold me."

He holds me very tight like that first time when he threw me off. He doesn't now. He is stroking my hair, gripping my head and moving his fingers around. He says my name just once. Perhaps he didn't. I so want him to . . . It must not finish, ever, I've got to make it last, I feel he wants it too, if only I could kiss him, his face, I want to kiss his face, his lovely silvery face, I'd give anything—I must not disturb this smooth feeling flowing along. My lips are so hot I'm placing his hand between them. All my blood is in my lips, there is nothing left for the rest of my body, my lips are curling round his hand—

"Get up!" He is white. "Get up!" Cracks it down

like a whip. "What do you think you are doing?" Tugs at his belt again . . . I must be careful. I must not get angry. Play it down, as the grown-ups say.

"I'm so sorry, I really don't know why I did that, please forgive me, but I felt so mixed up and sad, it was kind of you . . ." Kind!!! That's a very good word, that takes the sting out of this scene. I did play that well, he doesn't look angry any more, I've made a sort of escape for him, an excuse, it does not really matter with such a sad, mixed-up little girl, he did it out of kindness. I'm getting better and better at this. It's a school lesson, I'm learning all the time. Of course he's got to have an excuse, can't have his patients climbing on his lap, making love to him. That's what I was doing, wasn't I? And that's what he was doing to me too. Only it was not going very far, but what does that matter. He held me so close to him, as if he wanted no distance between us any more, as if we were one single person.

"I think I'd better go down, the Group is starting in a minute. It's important to be there in the beginning, don't you think?" I say. If only he does not cancel the private sessions again right now—"I do think the Group is good now with this new boy who likes his mother. It helps us all to talk about these things . . ." I'm rattling on, anything to keep him from saying that he doesn't want me to be alone with him.

"Yes—the Group is coming along fine, I'll see you down there . . ."

I'm champion.

I arrive in the basement just a minute or so before him. Loretta gives me one of those looks: "I know you've been up to something and I can guess pretty well what." But I'm in my armour, nothing can touch me, I'm in my shelter very warm and glowing and Loretta can go and . . . yes. Self-contained, that's what I am. Sounds like a flat-advert, but it's the best feeling I know. You need nothing, because it's all there inside.

Clive is said to be "out" and joining the Group to-day. He's had intensive treatment. I think it means "shock", we all think it does. It's not so special, they do it all the time, and it helps some people. And they are none the worse for it. Clive does not look much different from when I saw him last. Maybe his speech is a bit slower, and he can't remember some of the things we discussed, but he is much more settled altogether.

Everybody is calm and we talk as if we were sitting in someone's home, only more honest and no small talk about things which don't matter. Everything does matter—that's the difference. When Clive says, "I've got over my prejudice," we don't let it pass or make polite conversation. Someone says: "Which one—tell us." We really want to know. And he knows we don't pretend. That's the big difference. Down here you never pretend, all you say is as near the truth as you can get, or as you can make yourself go.

"I thought mental hospitals were for—for mad people." Clive is a little older than the others; he can talk very well, especially now he feels better, and he brings it out all in a rush. He probably thought when he was in there, it's not so bad, I can talk it over with the Group, and that made it easier.

"That's a stupid expression for a start. What does it mean—mad? It just means "ill", something doesn't work out with your body chemistry . . . That's what I think—the doctors don't always. But some do. And the place is not bad at all. The only thing is—you can't get out, when you are really bad, keys and everything. But then—nothing can get *in* either, it's a protection both ways. Nobody laughs at you or talks behind your back, it's all so matter of fact. I'm not frightened any more, even if I have to go back."

I can't imagine him going back. He's so sensible. And it's nice to hear him say, "How have you been, all of you?" I want to shout, I want everybody to hear that I've never been better, that not ten minutes ago I was on . . . Watch out now, this *is* private, it's so private that out of a million and a trillion people just two of them know. I still have not calmed down properly and when Loretta asks me after the session to go for a walk with her, I'm almost glad. I couldn't go home now, with all those little devils let loose.

One of them says very loudly: "I'd love to, Loretta, but I mustn't be as late as last time." He heard . . .

"What's up with you and the Old Man?" She doesn't waste any time.

"Old man—doesn't that mean husband? As far as I know . . ."

"Don't be idiotic. Has he touched you yet?"

I hate her, I really hate her guts. She makes it seem horrible and slimy, an everyday thing, which every man does and sees how far he can go, not this special paradise feeling. She is holding my arm just below the shoulder, this way it's easier for her to touch . . . That's it! She is jealous. She wants to drag it all down into the mud. I won't let her, I won't even talk about it. I manage a giggle. "But Loretta, you know I would not let anybody . . ." She is only too happy to believe; nobody but her is ever coming near me. She pushes me into a corner and throws herself on me as if she was starving. That's what I wanted to do a little while ago, I felt I was starving if I could not touch him . . . What *is* the difference? It's not what I do, it's what I *feel* when doing it. With her it's mechanic. Like a baby drinking . . .

If Tommy did that to me it would be unique, because it's him. I'll never get him to do that. I can always think it's him—no, no, don't, it makes it ugly. Loretta is all over me and says, "Come back to my room, darling . . ." "Darling", she said it like a boy. It puts me off completely.

"Not to-day, I can't, mummie is waiting for me. She keeps asking why I am so late all the time. You don't want to get me into trouble, she may take it into her head to collect me from the Clinic . . ." That rings true. She does not insist.

"Another time perhaps?"

Perhaps. I'm beginning to lie all the time, I notice. To mummie and Illo, so they don't worry, to Loretta, so she is not offended. And to Tommy, so he keeps on seeing me. Maybe that's how it is, everybody is lying to everybody else so things keep moving and don't break down.

twenty-one

LILIA has left school and has disappeared with her mum into the wilderness. Somewhere in Devon, I think. I had forgotten all about it, when I got a card "Feel marvellous, look enormous. Mummie is a peach. Am perfectly happy. Love Lilia." No address. When the baby is born, she'll probably give a big party and everybody will find it all perfectly natural. Again I envy her a bit, but wouldn't swop . . . not now. All I do becomes important, it makes sense, because I know he will listen to it. When I talked of a girl the other day, he asked me what colour were her eyes, and I could not say. Or he may say: what was the sky like, when you were walking in the park; or describe their voices or what they wore and even their gestures.

It makes everyday life so special. I'm watching all the time, so I can tell him. I photograph things in my mind and have it all ready when he asks me. I keep the sound of voices stored away, or the way the wind moves the grass and the trees. What our street looks like. It's a lovely street. You go along the main road, lots of shops and people and traffic that never stops and then you turn the corner and go down this winding lane, like in a village, trees on either side, the air is fresh and new as if it had not travelled all through the city, but comes straight from the sea.

I don't hear the clicking of the typewriter. Mummie may not be home yet. But she is. Sitting on her bed as pale as can be.

"I—I will have to go to hospital. You must look after daddy."

"But you are never ill. You can't be, you didn't go to the doctor."

"But I did, several times, it's not—dangerous. Only it's got to be done."

"What? What has to be done and when are you going?"

"Now. To-night, in an hour."

"You can't just go like that, what will Illo say?"

"He knows, I rang him. He'll be here any minute."

It should not be allowed, things shouldn't happen without anybody knowing. Who will do my food and wash my clothes and see to it that I get up in time? And what's wrong with her, anyway? Why can't she be treated at home?

"You can't operate at home."

Oh my God. Oh God. "What is it you've got?"

"Woman's trouble. It won't take all that long. I've given Ilsa" (the girl who comes in every other day to help) "a list . . . It's all there, shopping and everything; don't worry, darling, it's all taken care of. I've got you this . . ." She unwraps a parcel and gives me a new alarm clock. No mouse on it, just the dial, but it's luminous. "I thought the mouse needed a rest, she has done an awful lot of ticking." That makes me burst into tears. "You stop that at once," she says, "or I'll start too and we'll have the floods . . ."

Illo comes home, does not say a word and buries his head in his hands. For God's sake! She's not going to die, is she, she's just going away for a couple of weeks. Illo does not look up and says, "Tell me when you want to go." It's not a funeral—I know lots of people who had operations and felt very good afterwards. Jane's mother is always in and out of hospital and nobody makes a fuss as if she weren't coming back.

"Now—right now," mummie says gaily. "I'm just in the mood. Got to pack my make-up, though, can't have you visiting me and thinking whatever made me marry *her*? Oh and my dandelion coffee—they won't have that at the hospital. Evalore, don't forget to wash your hair tomorrow and I like roses best when you come to visit me . . ."

Illo carries her little case down the stairs. I follow them to the car and she kisses me. "I love you, darling, don't forget that."

They are off. That frightens me, that she said she loves me. She is coming back, isn't she? It can't be serious, she wouldn't have been so gay. Did she put it on? I've seen films where they pretend nothing is the matter, and then they are dead the next day. But mummie isn't old, it can't happen to her. What kind of woman's trouble? They didn't even say when Illo would be back. I hate not knowing. There is a little message pinned to my pillow, saying: "Don't worry, Evalore, everything is going to be fine, I know. See you in about three days. Daddy will be back for dinner."

That's sweet of her, that's like a—but she *is* my mother . . .

I can't go to sleep. I see some light under Illo's door.

"Can I come in. I feel so lonely." He's got his dressing gown on, dark red silk, it's beautiful—if only he wouldn't look so terribly sad. The night lamp is on and the curtains are drawn. I've seen it a million times, but to-day I feel I'm in a strange room altogether. It's so quiet. I'd rather hear them quarrelling . . . There is a plate with sandwiches, a glass of wine. He hasn't touched it. Hasn't even unfolded the newspaper. That's the first thing he usually does. Just sits there like—like someone from the Clinic. That same sort of hurt, withdrawn face.

Same sort of offended look, as if someone had punished him, or beaten him and it wasn't his fault. His almond eyes look reproachfully at me as if to say, why didn't you prevent this?

He tells me that it isn't as bad as they thought (why didn't they tell me, I belong to the family too) and the operation was going to be tomorrow morning. It will be all over by the time I come back from school. Ilsa will have my tea ready.

Now that I've got Illo all to myself I don't like it. I have an awful empty feeling and anyway his mind is with mummie all the time. "She won't be able to have any more children," he says. "Well, you replace a good dozen anyway," and he smiles for the first time. "Off to bed with you. We'll manage. Sweet dreams."

They were anything but sweet. They were horrid. Or rather one was. I was in a lovely garden full of roses. I could pick as many as I liked, because there was only an old man around saying: Help yourself, they have no thorns. I broke off dozens and dozens and they smelled heavy and sweet, I could not get enough of them, the more I picked, the more I wanted. The grass was high and tickled my legs and a soft wind swept through the trees and made them rustle. I started counting the roses, but I got a different number each time. I had to count and recount them, I had to, over and over, they did not prick me because they really had no thorns, but their smell made me dizzy; it wasn't all that sweet, it was rather sickly, and the petals started falling off, so I was just left with the stalks. Then the stalks withered and became brown and ugly. I threw them down on the grass and they crawled off, like worms, very quickly by the hundreds, crawling through the grass. Nothing dreadful happened to me but I woke up with the most awful feeling that nothing was worth while doing and I didn't even want to tell Tommy about it—just stay in bed and hide under the covers.

But then my new alarm clock went off with a lovely little bell and everything came right. I made some coffee for Illo and myself. He went off to his work and I went to school and the day was not as bad as I had feared.

He came back at six. "Evalore, will you make some coffee, please." Of course I will, but Illo need not have said it in this tone of voice, he should not have told me, he should have asked. He's on edge, of course; he has not rung the hospital yet. Not before seven, he was told. We are spending two hours together, but it's not very pleasant. There is not much we can do but wait. I always wanted to talk to him, but I don't find all that much to say. He's watching the clock and says yes and not now, whatever I ask him . . . "I can't visit her to-day," he bursts out suddenly. "They could let me look at her at least."

He does carry on. What is there to look at; he's seen her only every day for the last twenty years.

He could have thanked me for the coffee. It's ten to seven now. It feels like catching a train and thinking you'll be late, because you are stuck in the traffic. Illo looks terrible. Deep creases down the side of his nose. Nothing has happened, or we would have heard. He does not talk; why doesn't he say something? He puts one hand tightly over the other, pressing them together as if he were afraid. I think I'm looking at him properly for the first time. He *is* afraid, he's forgotten all about me, he just keeps his eyes on the clock, pressing his hands together so tightly his nails become white. Seven—he dialled so quickly he got the wrong number. Tries again. Listens to the voice at the other side, closes his eyes and says "Thank God."

I am glad and I want to comfort him and say: you see it's all right. But as I look at him I see that he is crying. Can't bear that. A grown-up man crying. He makes a horrible rough sound as if he had a sore throat. He takes me in his arms, but I am not happy at all. He only does it because mummie is ill, not because he likes me. He would have done it to anybody, just because he is so relieved. I'm asking him when we can go and see her. "I'm going to-morrow and then we'll both see her together the day after."

"Why can't I go to-morrow too?"

"She is not well enough yet."

They don't want me. I always knew it. If she is

well enough to see him, she could see me too. They want to be alone—it's only a pretext.

I'm going to the Clinic straight from school the next day. Not going to hang around in the empty flat or making coffee for Illo and be left behind.

The boy who likes his mother too much is in the waiting room. His name is Rupert. He's got a little moustache as ginger as his hair. And freckles. Looks funny on a boy. He's quite nice really. He understands right away when I tell him about Illo and that he is not so nice when mummie is not there. He is a little older than me; they are all older, I think I'm the youngest.

"Do you think I am too young for the Group?"

He does not think so. "You are very advanced, Evalore, you don't belong in a children's group, they would not know what you are talking about. I didn't believe you were only thirteen when I saw you first, but then I don't know much about young girls."

No boy outside the Clinic would admit that. See what I mean. They are honest in here. And they watch themselves and other people more, they try to understand. Once Tommy said that one does not have to make an effort to understand oneself. If one knows how other people feel—I think he said "tick"—that's enough.

Rupert wants to sit next to me in the Group, but Loretta does not let him. She says she always sits there and would he move. He did not insist—he's new. She looks really good to-day. Black jeans and a black shirt with a stand-up collar. So slim and that mop of soft fair hair. I tell her so and she says "mm" as if she was eating something marvellous. I'm not in such a good mood. Illo's fault.

"My mother is in hospital," I'm glad to be able to talk, "and I'm in charge at home. I thought it would be what I'd always wanted—"

"Isn't it?" Clive asks me.

"No, it's dull. And nobody takes any notice of me. It's not as if I was well, is it? I would not be here if everything was all right . . ."

Maria says something and then Richard, then Rupert. He is rather timid, but I think he is very intelligent, because he says very politely: "But you look all right, I wouldn't know . . ." He stops. He wanted to say: that you are a patient.

Gretl becomes furious. "Say it, say it out aloud," she screams at him, "why don't you say it. You would not know she is a p-a-t-i-e-n-t. What's wrong with being a patient? We are all sick, sick, sick, you too, Rupert, don't you know you are sick, or did they tell you some tale about how you are a bit nervous lately or a bit overwrought and you'll be all right in no time, if only you came to this bloody place just a few times . . . a few times! I've been for ages and I still can't . . . I can't look at—" Her pimples light up again and her glasses become steamy. She plants herself right in front of Rupert:

"You like a fifty-nine or a ninety-five do you, do you?" He does not know what to say. Numbers mean nothing to him. But Gretl gets more and more upset and shouts, "Who likes a fifty-nine, who likes a fifty-nine." I'd like to tell her I do, because Tommy is—fifty-nine. Why shouldn't I tell her, I'm upset too, why should I keep quiet; mummie is away and Illo is away with her and they don't mind how I feel.

"I do, Gretl. I love fifty-nines, they are great."

She turns on me: "You like them?" and more shrilly, "You can't—they're beastly!"

Stupid girl! A fifty-nine is just like any other number. I'll tell her, I want a fight, it would be very good to have a real rumpus. I *want* a clash, a battle: "It's the best number there is. Looks marvellous, just imagine a good loopy five and a . . ."

Gretl goes mad and comes at me like a prize-fighter, head lowered and fists clenched. Rupert tries to help me. He pulls Gretl away from me and her specs drop on the floor. There's a general pushing, everybody seems to join in, to tug and heave and dash about. Gretl flings herself on the floor, trying to find her specs, but they got crushed of course in all that upheaval and she howls like a wolf. "My specs, my specs, you've broken my specs, ooooooh—" We don't know any more why we are fighting and it becomes really nasty and people get hurt. Tommy pulls everybody apart:

"Break it up, do you hear, break it up at once!" He is so strong and his voice is so peremptory that we all get back to our seats rather sheepishly.

Only Gretl is still crouching on the floor, sobbing and picking up bits of broken glass.

"Gretl," says Tommy, "you've got beautiful eyes, do you think you could wear contact lenses?"

Gretl looks at him openmouthed, for a full minute. "Beautiful eyes? Me?" We all tell her how lovely her eyes are and does she think her parents could afford to buy the contact lenses because she never would need specs again and people could see how nice she really looks. She sits down on her chair, doesn't talk, but smiles to herself all through the evening. How clever Tommy is, how strong, the way he restored order and nobody was offended— I've never seen Gretl so happy.

"Do you feel like talking about the fight?" he asks us. We all think yes, it would be a very good thing to discuss. We try to understand how and why it started, that Rupert joined in to help and how we all got very angry and forgot or never knew what we fought about.

It gets late and Loretta says she is going to see me home. We stop on the way for a bite, she knows a place where they do a plate of spaghetti like nowhere else. She orders some sweet red wine to go with it—like a man. It's nice to be taken care of, especially when I'm so hungry after the fight and nobody expects me anyway. I'm sure Illo is still with mummie.

Loretta keeps filling my glass, it makes me so tired, I'm not used to it. She is nice though, doesn't try any funny business and says she can see I need a rest, pays for the lot and out we go. As we pass her place she asks me: would I come up with her, as she's cold; she'll show me where she lives and then we'll go on home, she'll just collect a woollie. I can't very well refuse. We climb up three flights of stairs, her room is at the top, rather nice and colourful with lots of posters on the wall, one of those Indian bedspreads and a furry rug on the floor. Half-ready sandals standing on a table and her tools. It's cute—funny, that's not one of *my* words. Wish I could lie down for just a minute. I'm flopping down on the bed and Loretta murmurs: so tired, poor little Evalore is so tired, and starts undressing me. I mustn't, I keep thinking, it's all wrong, don't let her do that, I don't want it, I don't—

She is shaking me. "Wake up, wake up, you must go home. What will your father say, it's after midnight . . ."

Illo is looking out of the window. "Where have you been? I just rang the Clinic, there was nobody there any more . . . where were you?" Serves him right. He can worry about me for a change.

"I had a meal with Loretta."

He isn't exactly satisfied, but he doesn't pursue the matter. He looks so exhausted, I think he can't be bothered as long as I'm home in one piece. He says mummie was still asleep, but she looked all right and the doctor said everything was fine and I can go and see her to-morrow.

twenty-two

GOT a lovely bunch of deep red roses for mummie. She will be pleased especially as she will feel terrible and look awful. She hates looking sick, the roses will cheer her up. She is all by herself in a little pink and grey cubicle full of flowers, her favourite picture pinned on the wall, a big shaggy lion and a gypsy in the desert. Somebody who looks less ill in a hospital bed than she does I couldn't imagine. She is sitting up in bed with two enormous cushions behind her back, a pile of books on the night table and a bottle of wine and a glass on a little tray on her lap. As if she was on holiday in a hotel. Got some stuff on her face I've never seen before, grins when I kiss her and says "Careful now, I'm all hollow,"—well! Cracks jokes with the nurses, gets a thermometer stuck in her mouth, gestures wildly, the nurse takes it out again, says good girl and leaves us alone.

"Roses are lovely. Just what I wanted. Like to try my wine?"

"No thank you." I'm off wine—for ever. "Why do you drink wine?"

"It's a pick-me-up, the best there is. The more I drink the quicker I'll be out of here. It's got to be Burgundy and I can have two bottles a day—nurse, can I have another glass—sure you don't want one, Evalore?" Illo looks at her all the time, beams all over and asks her whether she wants anything. Yes, she wants a new writing pad, she likes to put it all down, while it's still fresh in her mind and it's the best way to cure herself . . .

She *is* cured . . . I think she never was ill, she just wanted to get away for a rest. Then we have to leave the cubicle for a bit while two nurses go in and do things to her and she cries out and says: You want to murder me, you brutes. The nurses come out smiling and say she is wonderful and I'm a lucky girl. She asks me about school and the Clinic. Puts my roses in a vase and says: "Just took a pill, don't be surprised if I . . ." she is asleep and nurse comes in and tucks her up carefully. We leave the room on tiptoes. What was all the fuss about? I wish I were ill. Then everybody would be kind and Illo would come to visit me every day . . . That's a childish thought. I should be happy that mummie is all right and that it's all over. I am happy, I am very happy, if only she hadn't looked so—triumphant. As if she'd won a victory or climbed Mount Everest. I don't like her to be on top even in a hospital. It's not natural.

There is a film on TV and I'm sitting watching it with Illo like a married couple. It's no fun. I'd rather go to a film by myself or with Jane. Jane and I don't spend much time together any more. It used to be so nice listening to her telling me what went on in the car. I'm not interested in her stories now—it's always the same. The man takes her out, or maybe it's another man now—I couldn't care less. I've got my own stories. She doesn't find it so funny herself, she's got used to it. Maybe that's why she looks a bit sad—there is no thrill, no adventure, it's not *new* any longer.

Tommy is new every time. He looks different and he makes me feel different. It is never the same twice. Even if I repeat something, if I talk all about home, or my thoughts—I make new discoveries all the time. He is so still, not boring or empty, just very quiet, waiting for me to start. Shall I—shall I not tell him about Loretta. I've told him everything so far, on purpose, as he knows, of course. I want to force him—to force me. Makes it easier. That's it, that's what I'll do: "I've nothing much to tell you . . ." He doesn't react. "I said there was really nothing new except the visit to the hospital."

"Tell me about it."

"There is nothing to tell."

"Go on."

"I said there was nothing to say, why do you ask me to go on?"

"Maybe you'd like to talk about something else."

"No, I don't, there is nothing to talk about."

"Nothing?"

"Yes. Nothing—nothing that would interest you."

He sits in his chair, very remote, as far away as possible. I can't get connected. I've noticed one thing though: when I get really upset, when I let myself go completely he seems to come alive, to come out of his deep freeze. When I do exactly as I please it releases him in some way. I don't understand how it works, but it never fails.

I stamp my foot and scream at him without any reason: "It's not true—I've got something to tell you, come on, make me, it's your *job*, make me, make me!" Ah—I thought he would react. His dark grey eyes immediately focus on me:

"I can't make you if you don't want to. But I can't help if you don't talk. "

"I don't want your bloody help, I don't need helping, I just feel some things are better left alone ..." Hooked. He leans forward.

"Such as?" I am going over to the window and turn my back on him for a change. Without turning round, without raising my voice: "Loretta. I've been to her room." Bet he clenches his fist.

"Turn round, I can't talk like that." That's great—*he* can't talk without seeing my face. But it's me who is going to do the talking. Don't take any notice of him. "She is really very nice, she took me for a super meal after the fight the other day, wine and everything; she paid of course, she really looks after me, especially now that I'm all by myself, nobody else seems to care. She is a real friend—and her room is very nice—" Let's see, I'd better stop.

"Yes?" It does not make me angry any more, his one word act.

"Yes—what?"

"What is her room like?"

"Oh it's very personal, very secluded, she can come and go as she likes, there is a fur rug and coloured posters and her sandals . . ."

"Did you stay long?" That was a real effort. Should be rewarded.

"Ages. I even fell asleep, she had to wake me up it was so late."

He wants to know. I feel him behind me like a big wave coming to engulf me, but I'm holding out. Let him ask, let the doctor ask. I'm only here to be cured; I'm weak and helpless, I don't know how to behave, I am "disturbed", I don't have to say anything if I don't want to. I'm holding out, it's his turn—

"What did she—say?" That's not what you wanted to say, my darling, but I'm going to answer your question.

"She said my name over and over again." She did, I remember. She loves my name, works herself up just by the sound of it. I'd give anything to see what he looks like, what he feels. But I shall not turn round, unless he asks me to, because he can't bear it any longer. I hear him getting up and now he stands right behind me. My heart beats so much I think he can hear it. But I'm not giving in. Don't make a move. He takes a deep breath and goes back to his chair.

I'm still by the window, but now I turn round. He is sitting there, gripping the chair with both hands, eyes closed. His head thrown back in pain. I would die for him—I love him so much—but I still shall not speak. I've got to hold out, that's all I know. There is a movement in the room as if it was whirling round and round. As if there was a *thing* in the silence, a terrible struggle. I feel as though he's a young boy and I'm an old, old woman knowing what's good for him. He's got to break out, I'll drive him mad, I'll make him feel everything I do, I'll make him do it—speak, Tommy, speak—you've got to speak . . .

"Did you make love?"

"Yes. She did. I couldn't—I was too tired." The strict truth.

Still he has his eyes closed. "Why—why?"

Because I'm so lonely, because I don't get what I want, because I don't know. I do not know.

"Because she wanted it so much and there is no harm in it. It was the easiest thing to do." That also is the truth—why does it sound so wrong? He comes over to me, grips both my shoulders and pins me to the chair. Ah—the deep freeze has melted.

"I want the truth."

I feel so good I'm laughing right up at him.

"But Tommy, I would not lie to you, there's no point . . ."

"You lie all the time: you lie every time you take a breath, you little bitch!"

I'm a bitch, a lying little bitch. It sounds so tender I could—I am turning my head so I can touch his hands with my lips, not kissing him, just let my lips lie there. I am closing my eyes, I am perfectly and completely happy. There is nothing I want— just stay like that—forever and ever.

Oh, the—telephone, I nearly said it, although I said I would not. "Yes, speaking. Of course I'll take the Group as usual." No. He should not attend if he feels dizzy. "In ten minutes."

I let the others get on with it; I'm sitting all by myself, smiling idiotically—like Gretl the other evening. I'm hugging my knees so nothing will escape, I'll become a hedgehog, so nobody can touch me and take it away, a prickly, bristly, thorny hedgehog.

twenty-three

MUMMIE is home again. We are once more a proper family. It's all right for me, but how Illo can stand it, I don't know. Couples—ugh! the very word makes me sick. I'll never be a couple—half of it, that is—it's so tame. To begin with I would hate to have my meals always with the same person. "A little more sauce? Would you like some cheese? Was it all right? Would you like some coffee?"

All this sort of cosy munching together like a couple of baboons with napkins, disappear into their room, bang! close the door behind them and pretend it's natural, that's what everybody should do and if you don't, then you are not normal. If I think of all those millions and millions doing exactly the same thing every day of their lives—it makes me throw up. Cook, munch, munch, bang the door! I'll never never be like that. "Take your coat, Illo, it's raining." He is not a baby. Or "That tie doesn't go with your suit." Why can't he choose his own ties, he's a grown-up man . . .

I can hear their voices in the bedroom. I hate their bedroom voices, they are so unguarded, but I can't help listening.

"Can't you stop scribbling, Eva, talk to me; you had enough time for that at the hospital, I want to talk."

"No, I can't stop, I'll lose the thread . . ."

"You think your stupid writing is very important, don't you. Who cares?"

"So that's what you really think—I knew—I always knew, as long as I'm . . ." Blast, can't hear, I think they always know when I'm listening.

". . . good for"—Illo, furiously. Thud, thud, thud. Sounds as if mummie has thrown a couple of books at him and missed.

"Well, you'll have to wait quite a while, my sweet. Maybe I can lend you a fiver in the meantime, that'll see you over the critical ten minutes . . ." Can't follow. What does she mean? Why should she give money to Illo?

"Will you keep your voice down, you vulgar little slut, you know she can hear every word . . ."

"Let her, let her, as if it made any difference. There is precious little she doesn't know already."

"If you hadn't been ill . . ." Illo, through his teeth.

"What—what would you do, my darling?" Her voice is like treacle.

I know one thing—I won't become like that. I'll be special—I shall do things nobody has ever done before. I shall find out things, or maybe I'll explore new countries, only there are not many left to explore, they've been everywhere: I'll go to the stars, I won't be *ordinary,* that's the worst of all, a life where there are no sparks flying, where it's all settled. I won't be happy being dead either. I'll wake up now and then; see what happens in the world. Don't like things going on without me.

"Dornröschen" what a lovely word, the little rose pricked by a thorn—the sleeping beauty—she woke up after a hundred years. I'd love that, wake up every hundred years or so, see what it's like and then go to sleep again. I know, I'll become a scientist and I shall invent a drug so that you are not really dead, just sleeping and dreaming, then it starts all over again, only different.

It's very quiet in the bedroom all of a sudden. I'll have a look.

"Can I come in?" They look positively guilty. Illo is not undressed or anything like that—it's the look on their faces.

"Yes, by all means." He says it grudgingly, as if I had destroyed whatever they did before. "Haven't you any work to do," says mother of the red curls. Of course I have, but I'm not doing it. Why should I? I can get by without it. Mummie has lost her treacly voice—very stern and like a nanny.

"Yes, I have lots to do."

"Why don't you then?"

"I don't feel like it." That'll get her.

"It's not a matter of feeling, you just must accept that there are things which have to be done—no matter how you feel."

"No. I don't accept that. I do just as I please. You do too."

Illo flashes her a warning signal not to insist. I've seen it—as if to say, let her talk, it'll pass and she does not mean it anyway.

"That's different," she goes on. "I know what I'm doing, and I work all the time as you know. If I don't cook" (cook! she unfreezes a packet of scampi and bangs two pounds of fruit on the table) "I'm writing . . ."

"Writing is not work. You never go to the library and do proper research work like Walter. He works . . . you just play around."

"But Walter is a scientist. That's not the same. He's got to find out what's been written before."

"He is a writer" (mummie is only jealous because he gets every one of his books published right away, he is their best friend, that makes it even worse) "as well. Why don't you go to libraries?"

"I don't have to." She sounds like me a bit, not wanting to do my homework. "I just sit down at the typewriter and—and surprise myself. It's boring to work it out beforehand. If I know what's going to happen I needn't bother to write it. It's the discovery that counts, the sudden twist . . . The moment figures come to life and do as they please."

"Don't lecture, Eva." Good, Illo is bored.

"You see, mummie, Illo is not interested."

"You keep out of this . . ." They both say it at the same time. Ganging up again. I won't have this. I am always the odd one out, always alone. I'm *part* of the family. They have forgotten about me as usual, jabbering away, it hurts me, I'm going to make them take notice of me, me, me! not her all the time.

I'm starting to play with mummie's bottles and tubes. I hate each one like a person, the glittering green one, that's the one I loathe most and the perfume flask. What's she want to use scent for? It's artificial, as if you spread little drops of scent on a flower. It's absurd. Oh, it's a heavy sugary honey smell, I have taken the stopper off, it's like plunging into a hothouse, it's poisonous, this sticky stuff, sickly, shouldn't be used at all; I'm pouring the whole lot on the carpet, there, now the whole room stinks like a sewer . . .

"What on earth!" Mummie looks at the mess on the carpet. I think she is going to cry. I think she is going to throw a fit—just for a stupid bottle. The carpet soaks it all up and now there is a big yellow spot. They'll have trouble clearing that up. Mummie looks at it as if it were alive and could snap her head off any minute.

"It's all your fault," she says to Illo in that low

rumbling voice, which is worse than screaming right away. "You said I was lecturing, you always take her side. She does not know where she is, it's because we can't agree, that she does all those crazy things. You don't see that you have to be strict, that you must tell her . . ."

"*I* ought to be strict, that's the limit . . . How can I be strict when you don't give a damn; you never ask her what she does after school as long as you can sit and turn out your stories like a conveyor belt . . ."

"Ah," mummie advances on Illo, eyes gleaming, ready to strike, "ah—well let me tell you, whatever I turn out and however quickly it is ten thousand, a million times better than the trash you print in your paper, absolute muck, stupid, loathsome, boring muck."

"You don't seem to realize," Illo's voice is as cold and sharp as an iceberg, "that we happen to live on my boring muck, that I am generous enough to provide you with the means to sit and please yourself."

"*Generous*." Mummie's voice rises dangerously; she is losing control altogether. I don't mind them not taking notice of me, this is fun! "You—generous? Look at that!" She pulls at her dressing gown falling to pieces which she won't discard for the world although Illo's given her two lovely new ones. "Just look at it. I can find a man any day who'll keep me in this kind of luxury."

"But I just bought you . . ."

"Bought me, bought me. I wouldn't touch such hideous stuff with a bargepole. It's dull, do you hear, dull, dull, without the slightest bit of imagination, it's for a shopgirl" (mummie's ultimates sign of contempt, she's a bit behind the times, shopgirls look beautiful!") "Here," she pulls out the new gowns, rips them up right through and throws the bits into Illo's face—couldn't do it better at the Old Vic—"here are your presents, pink and blue." She spits it out as if the colours were an insult to her personally. "Why not polka dots, or a little neat white collar, that's more your style, perhaps you don't want to spend too much, or couldn't be bothered. I don't want your stupid things, you just don't know me, you haven't got the slightest idea what I like." She stamps on the bits and pieces.

Illo shrinks away from her, he doesn't admire her any more at all, he finds her disgusting. I suddenly remember the scene she made in the tram in Italy, screaming like a fishwife because of the boy who liked my legs . . . How jealous she—aha, that's what it is, she is jealous of me, because Illo told her off in front of me.

Illo is leaning against the wall, doesn't look at her and says sadly: "I can't cope, Eva, I can't cope with people who haven't found a mould, I'm not up to this, this unsettling hatred." He closes his eyes, a bit like Tommy when I've just said something really nasty. Then he says in a soft subdued voice: "I'll buy you another bottle . . ." The fool, the stupid fool! I hate him when he is like that. Like a worm, crawling to her . . . Yes! a couple—it's vile.

Mummie narrows her eyes, then bursts out laughing. She is mad. Why does she suddenly laugh, it's not cruel or anything, it's a gay happy laugh. "You are a nice boy," (boy!) she says, kissing him right on the lips. "Will you buy me a big new enormous bottle?" Can't stand this. I'm leaving the room. They can't be surprised if I'm not in a mould either . . . What can you expect with parents like *that*?

Quite glad that there is a Group session tonight. Would not stay at home for the world. It's unhealthy . . .

One of the rubber plants has died. It looks like a tired person with its arms dangling. I wonder why nobody bothers to take it away. Especially as the room looks always spotless, as if it had just been cleaned the moment before we enter. Not a speck of dust anywhere. The whole clinic is like that. Everything bright and polished. They probably have to keep it clean as it is a hospital, but all that brightness looks wrong. So much is stirred up here every day, so much poured out and spilled over that one almost expects it to show. It would be more natural if there were stains on the shiny black and white tiles and heaps of rubbish in the corners. It doesn't *fit*.

Bruno is back in the Group. I haven't seen him for ages. Of course we would all like to ask him where he's been and how he is now, whether he still makes love to himself now and then—but you don't ask this sort of question, unless he brings it up himself and wants to be asked. That's different. Loretta wants to be asked about herself, because she starts right away: "I'd like to change my doctor." Liebermann, the skunk, I remember. I certainly do not want to change mine—but lots of people want to, I know that.

Bruno says: "Who is your doctor and why do you want to change?"

Loretta: "Old smelly—he is not on my wavelength." That's a good expression, I must remember that . . . my wavelength.

Bruno: "Whom would you like?"

Loretta thinks it over for a bit. "I think I would get along with Dr. Manson." She would too: Dr. Manson is a woman—young and very nice looking.

Maria waggles her finger at her: "I bet you would get along—naughty girl."

Loretta does not mind. That's the good thing about those sessions. It's all taken for granted. Whatever you do, whatever you are—it's accepted right away, you don't feel you have to hide in a corner, because you are different. On the contrary, it's quite good to show the others how different you are. Then they come out with their bits and nobody needs to be *ashamed*. Our group is fine. That's be-

cause of Tommy. Everybody knows his group is
better than the others, people try to get in, but they
can't if they are too ill, only if they have started
getting better.

There is a new girl to-day. We don't know much
about her. Only that she had a breakdown. But
even I know that can mean anything at all. She is
pretty in a doll-like sort of way, with a round face,
a tiny nose, lots of baby curls bunched up on top of
her head. About fourteen, I would say, maybe
younger. She's got something in her hand, which we
are not supposed to see; she keeps covering it up
with her other hand.

Tommy says: "That's Janie, she'll be with us
from now on."

Loretta says: "What's that you've got there,
Janie?"

She takes her hand away as carefully as if she
were hiding a piece of gold. "It's my dolly." Her
voice—like a girl of five. High and flat, without any
real sound to it.

"What's her name?" We play the game immediately. If she says it's her dolly then we have to go
along with that. Janie says she hasn't got one. "I
just call her dolly."

"How old is your dolly?" Loretta goes on asking
her.

"I've had her ever since I was a baby," says Janie
in a different grown-up voice. "Isn't she beautiful?"

and she starts giggling as if she had made the funniest joke in the world.

"Why do you carry her around?" says Richard. It does not sound like a reproach, he just wants to know.

"I don't like to leave her at home, she would be lonely." Again that flat baby voice.

"I see," says Richard, "I understand."

"You don't understand at all," Janie seems upset, "nobody understands," and she bursts into tears. "I have explained and explained and they still don't understand, I want to make people see that it's not a game, and they don't see . . ." She dangles the doll by her two little plaits. "It's not a person, I know that, it's just that I think it could be . . ." she is sobbing loudly and we think Tommy will do something about it. But he sits still, just listening.

"And just how do you know it's not a person?" Maria snaps at her.

"She is not alive, she has no blood," says Janie quite reasonably.

"But you said she was lonely at home, only a person can be lonely," Maria insists.

"Only a person, only a person," Janie says in her baby voice. "Only a person can be lonely, very lonely always by herself, nobody to look after her, nobody . . . but I'm looking after her, I do everything for her, even if I go-away-don't-leave-her-here . . ." She does not separate her words properly, it all comes out in a rush. She talks like that for about five minutes, then stops, starts again and says it's all our fault. She is too ill, she should not be with us at all. She doesn't know what she is doing.

"Janie," says Tommy in a very distinct voice, "Janie, I could not hear, will you repeat what you just said. And will you cut out that baby-talk." That's not right. He shouldn't have said that. She can't help it, she doesn't do it on purpose.

"OK," she says in a perfectly natural way, "if you don't like it I won't do it again." During the whole session she stays like that. Talks normally, giggles a bit, but doesn't do that baby stuff. He knows his job . . .

"How did you know Janie was putting it on?" I ask him in my next private session.

He is wearing a new shirt and a tie to-day and a proper suit. I like him much better in his old blue shirt with the collar open. It's not so formal. Why would he want to dress up like this anyway? Is he going out to-night? With whom? His wife? Or has he got—no, he can't. He can't have a girl, he is a doctor. That's lucky for me. I believe they have to take an oath. He has to sign that book when he goes out. But surely not at night. He isn't the type, he wouldn't cheat on his wife . . . He is sitting right under the picture with the dark squiggles. I like it better every time I see it. It suits him somehow. Mummie would say it's his style.

"I know about Janie for several reasons," he says slowly in this marvellous deep voice he has when he

is absolutely honest and thinks about what he's going to say next. "The hospital that treated her
thought she was more or less cured. I've talked to
her several times, and," he smiles, "she told me, she
puts it on so that people listen to her better. There
was a time when she could not do anything else,
but that's past, she'll get on well in this group."

Love to hear him talk about his work. It's interesting, always new and different . . . "Tommy, do
you like your work?"

"What do you think?" I don't mind him putting a
question this time.

"I think you love it. I think you are better at it
than anybody else. I know you would even go on
working if you were ill . . ."

I'm stopping dead. What did I have to say that
for? He can't be ill—he is a doctor. Doctors are
never ill. Other people yes, and old peo— oh God,
he *is* old. I'm suddenly terribly, terribly afraid.
"Tommy," I say in a very small voice, "when do
people die?"

He gets up, comes over to my chair and pats me
on the head. "Not just now, Evalore, not now. I
haven't the time." He takes out his hanky and wipes
the tears off my face, real ones streaming down my
face at the very thought . . .

"Tommy," I'm sobbing like mad, "Tommy, are
you all right? Are you a hundred per cent all right
all the time?"

"Let me see, a hundred per cent? No, no, I can't

say that . . . There is a wisdom tooth giving me hell." I adore him, he is like a boy playing a game, he is not old at all, he is younger than me. "I can't swim for longer than an hour at a time, that's bad, and" he is looking at his hand, where there are very faint marks where I hurt him that time in the Park "I'm not as strong as I used to be when it comes to people attacking me without reason . . ."

He's never been like that before. I wish he would go on teasing me, there is nothing I like better. It makes us equal, as if he were a brother, only older . . .

"Are you afraid of death, Evalore?"

"I never think of it—for myself."

"But you've just thought of it for somebody else?"

"Hm, what happens when people die, Tommy, where do they go?"

"Why should they go anywhere?"

"They don't stay here, with us, I mean. They've got to go somewhere."

"But they are buried, or cremated."

"Yes, I know, but I mean their minds, they can't just disappear . . ."

"What is a mind?"

"A mind? I don't know . . ."

"Then how can you say it disappears or doesn't disappear, if you don't know what it is?"

"Everybody knows what a mind is, it's . . . it's . . . I don't know."

"Would you like to find out?"

"Yes. How do I do it?" My head hurts a bit, I can't stand up to this.

"What did you do when you were small and wanted to know something?" That's better. It's not so tiring. It's more ordinary, I remember . . .

"I once wanted to know what a flower is like inside and I picked a big yellow rose with my gloves on, because mummie said it's prickly, and I took off all the petals, there was a green knob inside, and then I took the knob off and squashed it in my hand and there was just a mess."

He laughs—but nicely. "There you are then, just a mess."

"Oh Tommy, why do you make fun of me?"

"Most minds are like that. What else can you remember?"

"I can remember lots of things, the more I talk to you, the more I do" (and don't you dare try breaking off, or I'll get terribly ill right away) "I can think very far back, very far . . . A beautifully laid table in someone's house with silverware and glasses and a very white tablecloth with lots of food and bottles. I came in from the garden, because I had just found a beautiful little worm, the ones that come out when it rains, and I put it on the shiny white cloth and everybody screamed and said I was a little horror and I liked them screaming and I liked the worm crawling across the cloth trailing a little mark behind like a drawing."

"How far back can you remember?"

"I can't say exactly, but now that we talk so often about myself, I think back to when I was three or four, maybe earlier."

I can see him becoming very interested. I haven't been in this outfit for nothing. I know where the journey goes. I am also beginning to see why I come here, I mean why they insist on me coming . . . That's what the treatment is for, isn't it? To make you see. I'm beginning to, Sir, I'm beginning to notice a lot of things, that's why I say: "If I weren't all the time afraid that I can't come and see you any more, I wouldn't feel so uneasy . . ." He is caught like a fish on a hook and does not even notice.

"There is no question of you not coming any more up here. You can relax . . ." That relaxes me no end. I'm coming over to him quite playfully, as if I wasn't really noticing what I'm doing, settle down on the floor beside him and put my head on his knees, holding on to his legs like a child. "Like to sit like that," I say, a bit like a baby, "wish I could always . . ." Suddenly I am on his lap. He grips my hair, pulls my head back and bends down. He hurts me again. He is not tender at all. But I don't mind, I don't mind, let him hurt me all he likes as long as he doesn't stop . . . don't let him stop . . .

Thank you, God, for making me ill, thank you for this lovely hospital, thank you for my doctor who

will . . . what? What does he really want from me?
He never touches me like Loretta. And the way he
"switches off" in the sessions downstairs . . . But so
do I, quite crafty, nobody knows, it's between him
and me . . . what a lovely thought. "We mustn't,"
he said, we, we, WE. It's not a couple, like mummie and Illo, We are just together and then we separate and when we meet we are both different, each
time as if I'd really not ever met him before. Does
he like me? I don't care whether he hates me or
likes me, or wants to hurt me, but it's me, me he
wants, he doesn't want his wife, I hardly ever
bother to think about her, she doesn't come into
this at all, let her have all her meals with him and
wash his socks, or maybe she doesn't wash them
herself, but she sees to it that they *are* washed, it
comes to the same . . .

twenty-four

"EVALORE, I said what is the largest city? Don't you ever listen?"

"Oh, I do, I do, largest city of what?"

"I don't know why you bother to come," says old Mississippi. "Turkey, it's Turkey we are talking about, for your information."

"Oh—Istanbul, of course."

"The position . . ." Haven't caught me this time, Bargy . . .

"On the Bosporus which connects the Black Sea and the Sea of Marmara, it's opposite the town of Uskudar" (which Eartha Kitt sings about) "the number of the inhabitants . . ."

"Stop, stop, I didn't ask you all that."

Those teachers. Can't do right by them. Now I'm doing too much. Looked it up on the bus on my way to school.

"So sorry, Mrs. Barge, I thought you would be pleased." Stupid cow.

"I am very pleased, I just wanted to have an answer to one question."

Teachers! They're worse than parents. Parents have got a sort of obligation, but teachers don't have to be teachers. Maybe they can't do anything else, and they think the kids won't notice if they are just about the limit. And it's all so slow. Names mean nothing to me. I forget them as quickly as I learn them. If I knew all the towns and all the rivers and mountains in the world and what the people do and what they send where and how much, I still wouldn't know what it's like. It's all wrong. You can't learn when everything bores you stiff. I never forget the things in books I like to read. I'm not ever reading kids' stuff with pictures and ponies on holidays and all that crap. I like grown up books where terrible things happen and it is all true, even if it's invented, and I can cry and be afraid and want to look at the last page like mummie with her German books.

"Well, keep it up," Bargy says. "You'll never get another chance when you've left school." The drivel she talks. I'll only get a chance once I'm out . . . I'll see for myself, not when it suits her, I'll *go* to Istanbul, while she still stands here talking about it, buzz off, buzz off. Oh, she gets on my nerves, "Keep it up— silly red face."

Looking round the class I see that nobody is listening properly. Some girls write in a listless sort of way. Some send each other little notes under the desks, others just gaze out of the window. I used to do that a lot. But since Tommy I don't mind the school all that much, it's something to get over with quickly . . . Then my real life starts. Meeting Loretta to-day.

I'd love to ask her up to the flat just once, but no, it would not be right. *Quatsch,* that's not what I mean at all, I mean that I couldn't get rid of her if I wanted to. And lately—I think I must finish this friendship. Friendship! Really. I started the whole thing in the first place to play up Tommy . . . Don't need to any more. And also—she's said everything in the Group. He knows. Why does he not ask me about her, when we are alone?—especially as that's what I said was the reason for meeting him again by myself.

I'm climbing up the three flights of stairs to her room. Each time the stairs seem higher and the whole thing more and more of a drag. I still find her pretty, I still like the moments when she strokes me—but the kick has gone out of it. She notices it too, tries all sorts of things, buys bigger presents. Mummie is a bit suspicious, I think. Well, she ought not to be—shows she has a dirty mind.

"Hallo, darling, you are all wet." I still hate it when she calls me darling. She takes my dripping coat off and spreads it out carefully over a chair. Coffee is all ready in the percolator. Hate that too. It's a *habit,* it's become one . . . That's horrid.

"I don't want any coffee, thank you."

"But you always like it after school, you said it wakes you up."

"Today I don't like it and I don't want to be woken up, thank you."

She looks at me anxiously: "Did I—say anything?"

"No, no, it's just that—have you got some wine?"

"I have no wine but," she smiles like a conspirator, "look at that, it's quite special." Not all that special, it's a bottle of whisky, scotch whisky. Got a little white horse on it on a black label. Tommy once gave me something with two red little horses on it; my heart goes stab, stab, I remember I nearly choked on it, but I'd take a cup of poison from him if he wanted me to—oh, Loretta, what am I to do?

"Whisky? That's lovely . . ." She is so pleased, I'm having two in quick succession. She is not so bad really. "Can I have another one?"

"Have the whole bottle if you like it so much."

I started giggling. "What—carry it home and say I found it on the bus?"

We find that terribly funny and start playing all sorts of games. She is holding my hand like a cup, pours the whisky in and drinks it up to the last drop. Then she says Evalore is a dirty little girl and pours it down my neck. It's cold, never knew whisky was that cold. She licks it all up and I don't mind any more what she does.

Still pouring with rain. I've got my black shiny mac and boots. Tommy hung it up the other day and said, was it French it looked so special. I like him hanging my things up, but I didn't like Loretta spreading it out on the chair like an old mother hen, having the coffee ready so I won't catch cold. She's tactless, she doesn't know what I like— Tommy does. He feels it even if I don't say anything.

"You look well, Evalore," Clive says to me in the waiting room. "I have a feeling you won't be with us very much longer."

That gives me a terrible shock. If I am too well, I won't see . . . "But I'm not well, I still have terrible nightmares and I don't work at school and . . ."

"They won't chuck you out just yet," he says.

It's fantastic what people here know . . . But he's made me afraid. I've *got* to be ill. I can't afford not to be . . . That's funny. I am looking at the fish tank and suddenly love every single creature in it.

"What are you smiling about?" I think we all have this habit of watching people's reactions and then ask them why they did what. Especially if you are in a group. It's a training, you know when somebody is lying, or when he wants you to go on asking, or when you should stop. It's like a code, when they tap out morse. I say I'm smiling because I'm looking forward to the session. It's not even a lie. I like to go, now that I know I can come by myself as well. They all drift in by and by. Gretl now wears contact lenses and she does look better. If only she would wash her hair. It's filthy and all tangled up, you can't even see the colour properly. I can't tell her that. It wouldn't make any difference; she's got to notice, or perhaps we could discuss it in the Group in a sort of impersonal way so she won't be hurt. Loretta doesn't like me sitting with Clive. Funny, but she does not seem to mind Tommy. She thinks it's all part of the treatment and all girls go for their doctor and it'll disappear as a matter of course. Well, she's wrong. It will never disappear . . . even when I'm fifty. Oh God, when I'm fifty he'll be—oh no, no, no, he'll be about a hundred. That's impossible, people don't become that old, unless it's in a village in Russia and even then it is unlikely.

I'm in a real panic. What if he says one day: "Well that's it then." Or perhaps they write a note saying that I need not come any more unless I feel worse. I've got to know. And it's perfectly true what Clive said. I am better. The fact that I notice it at all—that's a sign that I am. The dreams, the really bad ones, have almost stopped. I've started working just a little, ten minutes or so before school, and I don't look out of the window so much. There is just home and mummie spoiling things for me, but even that doesn't seem to matter so much, now I've got Tommy. I couldn't bear not seeing him any more.

Or do they leave it to the patients? Somebody

said the other day that *he* told the doctor he did not want to come any more and the doctor said, "Fine, that's what I have been waiting for."

Well, Tommy can wait till he is old and . . . I forget, I'm always forgetting. He is not old for *me*. I needn't think about his age. Why should I? I'm young and that's all there is to it . . .

But I won't leave anything to chance—I make sure.

The session starts on the dot as usual. Tommy is sitting in his corner. He's got a knack of melting away as if he was a ghost and then suddenly popping up when you least expect it. I look around me, Gretl, Bruno, Clive, Loretta, Maria, Richard, Rupert and the two new ones, the girl who talks so much about her father and the dolly one. Suddenly I feel a liking for all of them—I think they are the only friends I ever had.

Still, I've got to play a scene, I can't face the idea . . . it makes me go dead and grey and sick, sick. I think I'm going to be—I'm rushing out. I'm not sick but I thought I would be. When I come back into the room they all look at me and Tommy says: "All right?"

I'm only nodding, not saying anything. Might as well make the most of it. Well I felt sick, I didn't have to put it on, it came all by itself at the mere idea— "Would you rather go and lie down for a while?" Tommy asks. Doesn't he want me there? It's because of him I felt sick. He must know that. I suddenly hate him, really hate him, it burns me up just as much as when he . . .

"I will not lie down," I scream at him. "What do you want me to lie down for? I'm not ill, I'm very well indeed." Something besides the fury I feel tells me that I'm doing all right, that's how I must behave, if I want to stay on, just say anything, don't think, just scream . . . "You don't like me," I'm beginning to feel better, "none of you likes me, you think I'm disturbing the Group, you want me out of here . . ." Without any effort I'm crying buckets and buckets, oh that's right, that's the stuff . . . "Why don't you want me—I haven't done anything to you. At home they don't want me either . . . oh God, I'm so alone . . ." End of scene. I feel marvellous. While I'm still sobbing into my hands everybody says how much they like me and how can I talk like that, the group wouldn't be the same without me . . . I should think so.

Only Tommy doesn't say a thing. Again I get this Siamese twin feeling and I know—I know he's afraid too and he feels the same. "What will happen if she's well?" Only I can afford to scream it out aloud. "Nobody leaves this clinic as long as they don't want to," he says. "We haven't lost a patient yet," he smiles, "who feels he *is* still a patient."

That's that. He just told me. He knew what it was all about. I'm looking at him and it's as plain as anything on his face: I don't *want* you to leave. It makes me feel like an angel or a saint or somebody who can do miracles. Super-supernatural, that's quite right, I don't feel natural, I feel better than natural, off the ground, it's like flying all by yourself. I'm dreaming of how I will be to-morrow all alone with him. I close my eyes.

twenty-five

"IF the weather is good to-morrow, we'll take you to the Zoo." For God's sake, I'm not a bloody baby—"take you to the Zoo and show you the little teddybears and the funny monkeys." I was just about to say something very rude when I remembered Illo saying, "Why can't the three of us get on together?" He meant that I'm not really well. So I say, "That's very nice. Shall I put on my new dress?"

Mummie is pleased and says yes and if it stays fine we'll have lunch out, the three of us, and won't it be nice for a change with no friends. (Funny how every time we were going out there seemed to be a friend dropping in by chance, so we've never been out alone since the Italian holiday.)

What do they take me for? I know: it's a test. They want to see if I'm all right with the two of them. Wonder who thought of that. Bet it's not Illo—he wouldn't use a . . . a device like that. He

251

would just ask me. Typical of mummie, sly and round about and never to my face. She could have asked me. But no, "we'll take you"—I'm not a parcel! Wrapped in brown paper and tied up with a string . . . Isn't that how they carry bombs around so that nobody knows they are going to murder a king or somebody? I've seen it in the papers the other day, what did they call it . . . I really should read the papers, Illo always says I must know what goes on, not like mummie who only looks at the book reviews and doesn't know who is prime minister. Come to think of it, who is? And what did they call those little bombs they can make themselves and it doesn't cost much, but they're killing everybody; had a funny Russian name, something cocktails. Oh yes, Molotov cocktail, that's what I'll be.

The weather is fine, brilliant blue sky and sunshine. Just about five minutes' drive and Illo parks the car. He is wearing a coloured shirt and nice sloppy suede boots and mummie a silk dress, orange, you would think it clashes with her red hair, but it doesn't.

If I met somebody from my class now I would be quite pleased. I don't think their parents look so good. Mine look sort of enterprising, as if they did special things and didn't have a care in the world. They haven't—except me, of course, but then all parents worry themselves sick over their children. It's stupid. I won't be like that.

"Look at his eyes," says mummie as we stop in front of a tiger. He is beautiful, with a tawny orange colour, a bit like mummie's dress. He's got dark stripes, quite close together and they make a marvellous pattern. He hates his cage, I can see that. His eyes look a bit frightening, as if he would eat me if he could. I know tigers eat people. Just as well he's in a cage. Can't get near it, there's a large space between the cage and the people. So they can't feed him all sorts of muck. Yes, his eyes are strange. Fierce and glittering so much you can't tell the colour. As if he wanted to say, if I break out there won't be much left of you, you'd all run for your lives and it wouldn't help, I would get you all, every one of you . . . It's an odd feeling looking right into his eyes, I am like that sometimes, wild and boiling and hating because I can't get out. Don't want to leave the tiger. "Please mummie, let me look at him, he is so beautiful." Mummie nods as if she understood. We just can't tear ourselves away. I wonder what my mummie-mother thinks.

I watch the girls at school, the people in the group, Tommy, the teachers—but I never really have watched *her*. I do now. I see her watching the tiger, he looks at the two of us—we are three.

Is she happy, as a person, I mean, is she happy with Illo? She says you never can tell about other people's marriages. But I live with them and I still can't tell.

It's rather fun going from one animal to the

other and seeing how different they are. The bears
are nice and the giraffes. I like everything I see, I
like walking between mummie and Illo and they
don't talk to each other, they both talk to me all the
time and make sure I enjoy it. I feel sheltered and
happy and very young. We are having lunch outside and Illo asks us both what we would like best
and what about drinks. If only he had not mentioned the drinks. All was fine up to then. He *asked*
me and naturally I said I wanted some wine. Mummie looked grim right away and said it was too
early and I would be tired afterwards. She shouldn't
have said that. Always puts me in my place. I can
decide whether it makes me tired, maybe I like to
be tired and drift in a haze, and Illo said I could,
she has no business to interfere.

"You can have some at dinner, Evalore, then it
does not matter."

That's just it—it's too late to matter. It's no fun
then.

"I want the wine now, Illo asked me. I like red
wine, or a pink one . . ."

They exchange those telling looks: I warned you,
there you see what you have done, and now you've
spoiled it all sort of look.

"That's true, Eva, I did ask her, she is old
enough to know . . ."

"Ph! You are joking. You never think before you
speak," and so on and so on, why don't they get a

record player, press a button and have done with it. I can do it for them.

They start arguing: they positively enjoy it, bring it up to the sort of pitch when it becomes a quarrel, they say how they hate each other and don't know why they should stay together for another minute, everybody else is saying so too and why don't they divorce. And mummie is keeping the flat because of the view. By then they don't bother to listen to their own words any more and one of them says we seem to have run out of subjects, how about a coffee and would mummie like a fruit juice? Always reminds me of the sea when the waves are highest in the middle, then it goes up and down, they crash on the sand and there is just a little bit of foam . . . They don't mind their quarrels, it's part of their daily pattern, like breakfast. It's grotesque, but they often say "that was a good one" or "that never came up before" as if it was a game. More like a piano exercise with variations. I can always tell when it's going to stop with a bang, or with that bit of foam on the sand. I don't see the point of it. If I lived with someone I really liked, if I lived with—ooooh . . . I had forgotten about it . . . I'm not going to let anybody stop me seeing Tommy. I'm not well, they can't say I am well if I feel sick. "Mummie, I'll be back in a minute, I feel a bit odd . . ." Can just hear her start all over again: "There—I told you not to let her have wine at . . ."

Let them get on with it. They won't even notice

that I'm not there, far too busy working out their own problems. I've got one too. I must make sure. Tommy won't want me to go, I know that. But they may stop me and say I should do some homework instead, that I'm all right and it would be a waste of time and there is a queue of patients waiting. I am quite sure I would be worse right away if I couldn't see him. I am walking all the time, thinking what I could do . . . That's it, keep on walking, just keep on, out of the Zoo, past the car park, on and on, out into the street. Ah, that's good. My feet know better than my mind, they carry me off and away before I even think of it. I don't want to see any more stupid animals. I'd like an ice cream. It's true, my legs feel a bit heavy, I'd better have a coffee too, because I won't be going back.

By now they will have started one of their famous dialogues and whose fault it was in the first place. Perhaps they are a bit worried that I'm not back yet. Illo will be very calm and say, let's wait, she may have gone back to look at the tiger and mummie won't think so and will start getting nervous. Can't help that. It's what I want, isn't it? I want them to worry; I want them to think, she is not as well as we thought, if she wanders around like that without any reason. I'll go into a cinema and they won't find me there. Or into another coffee bar and have a piece of cake . . .

"Would you like another one?" a boy asks me;

he looks a bit like the one in the tram in Rome, only he is English.

"Yes, I would——" Why shouldn't I? It's kind of him to ask me. He buys me a lovely big creamy one and says it's a pleasure and am I waiting for a friend? I say I'm not and look properly at his face. He's all right, but I don't like his smile although he's got lovely teeth——his lips are so full and red and just a bit moist.

He is not a boy, he is a man, over twenty I think. He shifts around a bit and says do I like records? Oh Lord! I know that one——he's going to say which one best and he happens to have it in his room. Don't like his hands either. His nails are too long and look as if he had them "done" at the hairdresser's. Tommy's hands are beautiful, I love his hands——why can't he sit here with me . . . This chap has got a vulgar sort of voice, he tries to make it sound soft, but I know he's really horrid, I'm far too young for him.

"I'd like another cake." He goes and brings a smaller one this time, mean little squirt. Who does he think he is? Just go and admire his records for one and a half pieces of cake? I would not go with him anyway, I don't go with strange men like Jane. It's not——interesting. Do I like the cinema? He knows one nearby where they play lovely X films. I've heard that one before too. Stupid ass——can't he think of something better. The more I look at him the less I like him, although he's dressed very well, but everything matches as if he's spent hours and hours choosing the right colour to go with his eyes. Wishy-washy blue, like my ink bottle when it's nearly finished and I pour some water in to make it last. Can't he see I'm not interested, just want to kill some time. No, he does not notice. Look at his ring! It's a diamond or something very expensive, but his fingers are so bulky it's embedded in the fat, he could never take *that* off.

Puts his hand on my arm, as if his miserable cakes give him the right. "Shall we go for a little stroll?"

"I'd like to very much, but my parents . . ."

"Your parents?" He begins to frown. "What have they got to do with it?"

"They told me never to go out with anybody before I'm fourteen even if I know them and I don't know you and . . ."

"You're not even fourteen?"

I open my eyes really wide and shake my head three times very strongly like a little girl.

"Thirteen," I say and make it sound like five. Then I push my lower lip out and start biting it. He's gone and across the road in no time at all. That was easy. I could make a living this way. It's nice to look older and then give people a scare.

Wonder whether I should go home now, or give them a ring. After all, they tried to give me pleasure by taking me out and—no, I think I'll wait a bit, then they'll ring the Clinic and ask have I

been there, or do they know where I could be . . .
That's just what I want, let them ring the Clinic.
They are bound to.

Now I can do as I like I don't want to go anywhere. Could go and see Loretta. She'd love it.
She'd let me stay as long as I like. That's a bit
much, and I'd hate to sleep with her in one bed
squashed against her all night. Suddenly I'm starting to cry. It's not much I want, is it? Just to go on
seeing my doctor when I'm not well.

They are in a real state when I open the front door
and run up the stairs to the flat. Mummie looks as
if she was going to throttle me like that time in
Naples and Illo is so worried he can hardly speak.
"Where . . . where have you been all this time?"
He doesn't open his mouth properly, squeezes the
words through his teeth.

I've thought it out very carefully. "I feel awful,"
I say in a very tired voice and I'm going straight
into my room. They both follow me. Lying down
on my bed and close my eyes. Then, bit by bit, "I
felt so dizzy so I thought I'd go for a quick stroll
that would make it better, then I lost my way and
went round and round and when I came back to
the table you had gone. . ."

"We looked for you everywhere, then when we
came home and did not find you, we rang the
Clinic."

Ah—I'm not stupid. "The Clinic? What for?"

"We thought they might know."

Then I'm sick—really sick. The lunch and the wine and those vile cakes. Wish I hadn't eaten the last one . . . Mummie puts her cool hand on my forehead and says no, we don't need a doctor, I have no temperature and could Illo ring the Clinic and say I am back, but not too well.

I think I am a bit of an actress after all. I did not *have* to run away from the Zoo. I remember when I felt much worse, when I *had* to do things I did not really mean to do, something inside was driving me, like Gretl when she can't bear the fifty-nines, or that time when I was with mummie on the chair lift—no, I won't think of these things now. Illo always says one can only be truly happy with a real healthy bad memory. Still, I know I was sort of trapped then, everything was coming on top of me. I know—I was like a fly in a spider's web. I once saw this happening in a hotel room right over my bed. It was terrible, but I could not tear myself away from it: the fly being wrapped up in those thin sticky threads beating its wings. It was horrible, but I had to look till the end. It made me so sick that I couldn't eat afterwards.

I'm not a fly any longer. Rather a spider, although I don't eat anybody. But I do wrap them up. It's naughty really, it's cheating—still, I'm all right now and it's a lovely feeling having mummie sitting by my bed watching over me and my pink lamp on, which makes my glass animals look all rosy—instead of tramping the streets and meeting squalid men with thick fingers and diamond rings . . .

"Whatever happened?"

"I—I really don't know, Tommy, I can't remember . . ."

"You went to the Zoo with your parents?"

"Yes, and I liked it very much."

"What did you see?"

"A beautiful tiger and giraffes and lots and lots of other animals."

"What did you like best?"

"The tiger."

"Why was that?"

"He isn't—he hasn't given in."

"Can you describe him?"

I tell him every detail, how he looked and how I felt with mummie next to me and thinking whether she was happy.

"What then?"

"We had lunch and Illo asked me whether I would like some wine." Then I tell him all about the quarrel and how they always do it till it becomes so boring.

"What did they quarrel about?"

"Me: whether I should drink wine at lunch."

"Do you think you should?"

Needn't lie to him. "No, I shouldn't during the day. It makes me so tired."

"Is that why you were sick?"

"No, it was the cakes."

"What cakes?"

I tell him I got lost and I couldn't find the table. He doesn't believe a word. I'm glad. Wouldn't have thought much of him if he had.

"Where did you have the cakes?"

"A man bought them for me." I say that very loudly.

"Tell me——" That was not a doctor's voice. Nothing wrong with my ears. That was a man's voice wanting to know about another man. I describe the man and his chubby hands with the ring.

"Did you like him?"

"Like? I could just about have murdered him when he put his hand on my shoulder. You should have seen him bolting across the road . . ." Can't stop laughing.

"Why did you send him away?"

"I didn't——he just ran for it——when I told him my age."

"Do you often——speak to men you don't know?"

"Never, ever . . ." I'm coming towards him and stand between his knees, looking into his eyes, saying like a child, "I don't like strange men, not even to talk to, I like to talk to you . . ."

He pulls me into his arms. As soon as he touches me I go up in flames. So hot, I can't bear it, must open my dress——

"Don't," he cries out, but it's too late. For the first time he's seen me, the real me, what I look like. He walks to the door like in a dream, turns the key and takes me back into his arms. He hurts me all the time with his hands, with his lips.

I don't cry, I don't make a sound, he can do what he likes, even if he—he hurts me more and more, but it's good to be hurt like this. Why does he suddenly stop?

"Oh God," he moans, "I mustn't . . ." and turns away from me.

My dress is closed and I say, "Don't you like me?"

He says nothing for a while. Holds on to the chair with both hands, lets his head sink very low and says: "I do."

I am married to him.

Lovely world. School is lovely. Tuddyfoot is lovely. Barge is lovely. He said it, he said it. I like Miss Pringle, I like the grey buildings and the cracks in the wall. Istanbul is a beautiful town—maybe he'll take me there and we'll get lost in the little streets and never come back and everybody will say whatever happened to Evalore and soon they will all know . . .

twenty-six

I knew it—I said so. Lilia had thrown a party to present her son to the amazed public. Reporters and all, headline in the local paper, a picture of "thirteen year old mother".—looks more like twenty with a marvellous dress and lots of bracelets—holding her baby tenderly and gazing at it in admiration: a modern madonna. I don't even think she did it to drive her former teachers up the wall—she just enjoys the whole thing. We are discussing it in the Group to-night.

I still admire her—as one admires something one can't and would not do oneself, but which one envies all the same.

"Let's discuss 'envy'," I say in my grown-up voice to the Group. Stunned silence. Tommy's attention is immediately aroused. That's something new. It's not personal. It's not "I did this and she did that." It's different, it's abstract. Good—I like to be different.

265

"Are you envious?" Gretl asks. That's not what I want. Blow those personal questions.

"I don't think Evalore meant it as a personal topic. She just wants to know what you think of the emotion itself."

Yes, Tommy, yes, that's what I mean. Why don't we go somewhere quiet and discuss it by ourselves . . . and I love it when he says my name. He does not say it like mummie or Illo, a word which has been used a thousand times. He says it carefully and pronounces every letter, as if he was discovering it just now and liked the sound of it.

It's very difficult to talk without bringing your own feelings into it. We can't keep it up for long. Rupert makes the most of it and says how he envies all grown up men and he hates them for being so sure of themselves. Gretl envies all pretty girls. But I want to know how they feel about being envious altogether. Not when *they* envied somebody.

In the end it becomes a free for all and we are airing our pet envies. When I least expect it, Clive suddenly turns on me and says: "Why did you start that discussion, what's the point—and whom do you envy?"

"I envy all the girls . . ." I begin very slowly and deliberatley, "all the girls who are loved by a man, not a boy, a real man, a brave man, who does as he pleases, who does not live like other people, who makes his own laws" (I feel very proud of that bit) "and doesn't give a damn for what other people think. He would not be a miserable little ant, crawling about in a heap, he is a king," I say very loudly. "That's the kind of man" (I must get back to "envy" somehow) "I mean that's the kind of girl I would want to be, to have a man like that love her . . ." Suddenly I see Tommy with a golden crown standing on the steps of a castle and the people far below looking up to him.

Clive says: "She's off."

Tommy feels uncomfortable. It is as if I were sitting right inside him and felt all his feelings, he's going to get us off the track, I know . . . "Lilia's party," he says.

See—now we want to find out whether it's terrible for the baby to grow up without a father.

Richards says: "It isn't—with heaps of money."

Gretl says: "Or when you have none at all."

We get stuck for a bit. Until Maria says she wants to speak about something strange that happened to her. When somebody speaks in a low hesitant voice, it's important. Then they have thought about it a lot, don't know what to do and present it to the Group . . . either because they want to or because it comes out when they can't keep it to themselves any longer.

She has met a man who has seen her in the Clinic when she was very ill and undressed all the time. He was a patient too. But now he is cured—well, more or less—and doesn't come any more except once a month for a check-up.

They like each other very much and meet often. But he has never once put his arm around her and she would give anything if he did. He says he can't, because he has *seen* her and it puts him off. Now she feels she is getting worse and should she stop seeing him altogether? We all noticed she was getting worse. She is terribly tense, can't keep her hands still and says things we know can't be true: people at the school behave oddly, they don't want her there, or her friends' parents don't invite her to parties, this kind of thing. We all make up stories often, but then we admit we do, as soon as we are found out—and don't mind. She gets absolutely beside herself with fury, if we say we can't believe her.

"What do you feel like doing?" Richard puts it like a doctor.

"Hitting him," says Maria. "He is stupid."

"What do you like about him if he's stupid?" Gretl asks.

Maria beams like a lighthouse. "He is so good looking . . ."

That's a joke. He is a horrid little slug with a turned up nose and hair plastered down with cream. They don't come more horrible. What can she possibly see in him?

"He is so clean and never says a coarse word. I never met anyone like him, he is marvellous." She's in a trance. Just goes to show.

"Why don't you ask him?" Bruno suggests. "Ask

him whether he's a . . ." he quickly looks around to see whether anybody would be offended, decides no, there is no one like that in the Group, and goes on "whether he likes boys."

"Oh I couldn't," says Maria, "it would shock him too much."

She's nutty. We all know the man has been in prison for rape; he's never been in our Group, far too old, and then he would not fit. She is so innocent—but then so am I. I've seen and heard so many things which you only read about in the Sunday newspapers and it doesn't make a scrap of difference. Been with Loretta, out with a couple of boys—it doesn't touch me. I think I'm not really there unless I'm with Tommy.

We speak all the time about the most intimate things, but I don't change, I mean, I don't feel or behave differently because I know so much. I don't forget about it like a lake doesn't forget the trees and the grass that are mirrored in it. But the lake does not change. Maria's problem does not get sorted out, of course, at least not to-day. But she becomes happier talking about it. I noticed that: talking in the Group takes the edge off things. It doesn't blur them or anything like that, but the very fact that we *can* talk makes them better, they get an airing like an old blanket.

Still can't understand Maria. The chap she's mad about looks so ordinary. That's the worst one can say of anybody: ordinary. Or maybe she's attracted by his past . . . hopes he'll do it to her; no, that's a nasty thought.

"Maria, why do you think you are getting worse?" Tommy brings us back to her.

"Because the headmistress told me she does not want me to come to school any more—so I must be getting worse."

This sounds very odd to me. Maria is older than I am and next year she is going to prepare her O levels.

"When did she tell you?"

"Last week." She is not quite sure. "Or the week before."

"Why does she say you should not come to school?"

"Because I look too pale, because I work too much and can't sleep properly . . ."

We ask her why she doesn't take sleeping pills or tranquillisers.

"I do take them," she says, "but I still can't sleep."

Now we go into a sort of consultation and you would think you have a bunch of doctors in the room. There is not a pill we don't know. We also know how much you should take and which pill is best for what.

Maria shakes her head and says pills are no use, she knows she is getting worse and that nothing can be done about it.

"You want to get worse," says Clive, then he

adds something we all know, "You probably need to get worse, it's good for you."

Sounds crazy, but that's how it is. When you let go completely, and really behave as you feel you want to even if it looks mad from the outside, then you have a chance of geting better. I think I'll be a doctor, like Tommy.

"It's good for me," says Maria dreamily and begins to take her shoes off. Nobody says anything. Then she peels off her stockings. We say nothing and look at Tommy. Will he touch the little bell under his chair?

"Maria," says Gretl, "you know you should not do it."

We forget about Maria for a moment and discuss whether she should or should not go on undressing. When we look at her again she is just pulling her dress over her head, a nurse is coming in and leads her away very gently.

We look at one another and feel afraid for a bit. Each thinks, it could happen to me, I could fall back suddenly . . .

"That's a shock," says Tommy, "one is afraid . . ." He is so good, so honest, he knows exactly when to speak and when to be quiet.

"I am afraid," says Bruno, "I am afraid so often . . ."

"Me too," says the boy who likes his mother, "I think something horrible is going to happen any minute. I wish it would, then I need not worry any more."

Each one says how he or she feels. It's odd, but it's like taking one's temperature, only we do it by thinking, by plunging right down to places where you normally don't go. When I'm grown up I shall be more grown up than the others, the ones who've never been here. I'm not sorry really that I was . . . not was, *am* ill, I still am ill . . . or I would not be here.

Loretta and I are sitting in the Park in our corner by the lake.

"Why won't you come up any more?" she asks me.

"I have to do my homework, I just haven't got the time."

"Haven't got the time?" Her voice is very shrill. "Don't give me that crap. You just don't want to be alone with me, do you? You want to be fooling around with that old gargoyle."

That was very nasty. She needn't have said that.

"What do you mean?"

"What do I mean—what do you think I mean?" Her voice becomes really unpleasant.

How could I ever have thought she was pretty? She's got a sharp little face and, anyway, I don't like that tone of voice, I don't have to say things I don't like saying . . . to anybody.

"I'm not blind. You go up those stairs and you come down as if you'd been given a million."

That's just like Loretta. She thinks money is everything.

"A million?"

"Don't repeat my words so stupidly. I know that bastard is up to something. I passed his door the other day" (I bet she didn't pass it, she listened with her ear pressed against the door) "and I couldn't hear anything. Nobody spoke—you are supposed to talk to your doctor . . ."

I don't say anything. She knows. I went with her in the first place so that she would talk about it in the sessions.

Suddenly she smiles at me and says: "I think I'll report it to the Hospital, a little enquiry can't do any harm."

I could have killed her on the spot.

She goes on smiling: "Unless you prove me wrong, of course."

That's blackmail, but I can't complain about it, because that's exactly what I did with her; I remember I said I would not ever go out with her if she didn't talk about it afterwards in the Group.

"How—how can I do that?"

"Come up and I'll tell you."

She seems to like me even better now that she knows I don't want to come any more. She tears my clothes off and throws me on the bed. "I'm better than any man," she says and kisses me like mad, "any man, clumsy brutes . . ."

I hate her, I hate her, I wish it was Tommy, I wish . . .

I close my eyes and it *is* Tommy, why did I never do it before; I can see him so clearly, it is as if he were right here with me. I hear myself moaning with pleasure, Tommy . . .

"You bitch!" She throws me off the bed. "I heard you!"

I must have said it aloud. I thought she would not notice. She hardly gives me time to put my clothes back on, flings my shoes out on the landing and my satchel, kicks me out and sneers: "You just wait—that's not the end of it!" bangs the door shut and I'm going down the three flights of stairs which I will never see again. I'm upset, naturally—but oh, so relieved. She won't really do anything to Tommy. People would want to know what business it is of hers; they won't believe her in the first place. She is a patient—you don't believe everything they say. Half of the time they make it up, we all know that . . . Still, it makes me uncomfortable, apprehensive . . . Should I tell him about it? But then I would have to tell him the whole story. He knows quite a bit, I wanted him to in the beginning—but now . . . Life's so tricky, things always get out of hand, and I can't ask anybody. Can't discuss it in the Group, can't tell Illo. I'm on my own—for the first time.

The session is almost over when Tommy says: "I have an offer to go to the United States. I have accepted it. We shall have three more meetings and then you'll be rid of me." He does not look at me, stares straight in front of him. I don't hear what the others say, I don't see what they are doing, I only know I have to get out of this room, this black black room . . .

A nurse slaps my face again and again. "Evalore, Evalore, open your eyes." I am lying on a couch and there is a wet flannel on my face. "Better? Colour's coming back to your face. Still dizzy?"

"I'm all right now, thank you. No, I'm not dizzy any more, must have been the heat or the new pills. No, I don't need a taxi, I'll go by bus—I'm fine, really, don't worry." She sees me out. I'm doing everything I usually do. I walk up the street to the bus stop, waiting a little, then I'm sitting down and pay for my ticket. Get out and walk up the hill.

"Hallo mummie, I'm a bit tired . . ." and go straight into my room. Start tidying it. Never get the bedcover straight. All those books on the floor. Pick them up one by one and put them on the bookshelf. And the clothes in a heap on the carpet. Mummie is quite right, I should hang them up, they look crumpled, as if I'd had them for years.

Then I straighten out my glass animals. It's nice to have them all in a row. There is no more to do, so I'm starting my homework. Can't remember when I ever did so much in one go. First Maths, then French, then History. Write it down so I won't forget. That's done too—what now? Bottom drawer in the chest does not close. I tip it on the floor and start folding everything and put it back. There is a cellophane bag under the woollies. My dress, my white dress, the spot Tommy tried to rub out . . . No, I'm not going to faint again, I won't let myself. I'm gripping the bag as if my life depended on it. I am putting it under my pillow, it's safe there. I tell mummie that the new pills did not agree with me and would she let me stay at home to-morrow, I'll go back to school the day after. I'm showing her my homework, so she won't ask me any questions, and she says it's all right and don't forget you have a private session to-morrow.

twenty-seven

IT does not stop raining. I'm in bed watching the drops beating against the window. I am alone in the flat. It's very quiet except for the wind shaking the branches of the tall tree in the garden. There is a tray with food by my bed but I won't eat anything. Another hour and I will have to get dressed to go to the Clinic. My body is very cold and it feels as if the blood has stopped running. Pictures drift through my mind like bits of film, quite clearly, I even hear voices talking. That's what happens when people are drowning . . . I can't hear my own voice, I am not in the pictures either. Once I saw a huge glass tank filled with water on TV, the swimmers danced a sort of ballet in the water and the public sat behind glass walls. It's like that—a glass wall between me and the people moving about in my mind.

The noise of a plane passing, birds crying in the rain and now and then the clock from the steep green church-tower strikes. Five o'clock now—I must get up.

I'm smoothing the sheets, patting the pillows like I saw Ilsa doing and cover the bed carefully. Doesn't look like my own room—it's so neat. I push the chair under the table, straighten the pile of books on the shelf and look around once more. One of the glass animals has toppled over, a little brown deer with long antlers. I must put him on his feet again.

I should have taken a scarf, it's still raining. Too late now, I won't go back. It's pleasant to feel the rain on my head like a soft shower. It's good for the hair, it makes it shiny and it starts to curl a bit at the ends.

"Go right up," says the girl at the desk, "there is nobody with the doctor now." It is a great effort to walk up the stairs. My boots leave dark wet marks on the blue lino. I'm counting each step so I won't notice how steep they are. I am so weak, better hold on to the bannister. Is this how people feel when they are old? I open the door without knocking.

Tommy does not sit in his chair. He stands in the centre of the room, very straight, the palms of his hands flat against his thighs like a soldier. He wears the dark blue shirt open at the neck. But I cannot see the scar.

"I could not tell you before, I could not—I did not have the courage . . ." he says and waits. I am nodding to show him that I understand.

"I *had* to accept it, I've got to leave, don't you see . . ." He waits again for me to speak. I am nodding once more.

"You hair," he says, "it's soaking; you should have taken a scarf, it's been raining all day, you'll catch cold."

He takes a towel from the washbasin in the corner and starts drying my hair. I like him doing that, watching while he wraps the towel around the long dark strands, rubbing them with his hands.

"Let me take your coat." He hangs the dripping black coat up on the door and says in a new harsh clipped way, "I'd better turn the fire on." He bends down, turns it on and warms his own hands in front of it. There is a slightly dusty smell, because it's summer and it has not been used for a long while.

He sits down and looks at me for the first time this afternoon.

"Oh no, oh no!" he cries out as he sees my white dress with the large red spot. "Why did you put that dress on, why?"

I cannot answer that. I don't know why I put it on. It seemed natural, I did not have a choice really, I had it on before I knew I was doing it. I shrug my shoulders. I cannot tell him, there does not seem to be a reason for doing it.

"Speak to me," he says, "you've got to speak to me."

He is pleading with me as if I was his age, as if I was his equal—or perhaps he hopes that I might tell him that everything is all right. But I cannot speak, because nothing is right.

"Evalore," he says in his new clipped voice, "speak, say something . . . you must, you must." He becomes quite urgent. It seems awfully important to him. This is what people come here for—to speak. He is very pale. Tries once more:

"If you don't speak I cannot explain . . ." He says my name several times, each time a little louder, a little more threatening. I am still standing and he gets up too and stands right in front of me, gripping his belt with both hands.

I am starting to smile, because he cannot make me speak. I am shaking my head and the white towel which he had wrapped round my hair falls to the floor. It's now very warm in the room and my hair is nearly dry. I am looking into his eyes and see the fire reflected in two red spots as if his eyes were glowing. Grey eyes with a red centre. He grips his belt with both hands and while I am still smiling, he undoes the buckle. I can see the leather slipping through the loops. He is lifting his arm holding the belt and makes it come down on my legs. It hardly hurts because I am wearing my black rainboots.

Then he starts hitting me all over, lifting his arm again and again. My skin burns like fire but I do not want him to stop. This is what I came for, I know that now. The skin on my arm bursts and little red drops fall on the dress. When he sees the red drops spreading he goes mad and hits me so hard I cannot stand on my feet any longer. I am kneeling on the floor. I don't quite know any more where I am, but I know it must go on till I forget everything. I must forget Loretta and Illo and the school and the Clinic and I must forget that Tommy is leaving and that Tommy is hitting me, perhaps he wants to kill me, that would be very good, but you can't kill people with a small leather belt; now I don't feel him hitting me any more although I see his arm moving and the belt swishing down all the time. Suddenly my head is very clear and I see his pale pale face, I see his bones like a design under the skin and the dark grey eyes with the red light in the middle . . . Poor Tommy, he must be very unhappy, very sad. Maybe he wanted to love me properly, it's not his fault, that's the way he is made, he can't give much else to a woman—a girl—only this crazy despair, this pain and hurt. Is that why he became a doctor? To find out about himself. When he can let himself go and make people suffer, suffer because of him. That's his way of making contact—his only way.

As I look at him, his madness goes, he lets his arm sink down, the belt drops and he suddenly folds like a pocket knife and crumples up in his chair.

I am getting up from the floor, take my coat from the hook by the door and slip it on. Tommy still lies in the chair, does not move. His blue shirt

is wet and clings to him everywhere. I can hear him
breathing so hard that I think he might be crying.
But I can't be sure as he is hiding his face. I want
to leave him now, it is not nice to see him like this.
He looks so untidy, I'm not used to that. I feel very
sorry for him, lying there with his knees drawn up
and this hard breathing shaking his whole body.
Perhaps I ought to speak now and say something to
calm him down. I could say that I did not mind
him hitting me. It was the right thing to do. For me
it was right—but not for him. It's better to say
nothing.

I am just putting my hand on his shoulder
and let it lie there for a moment . . . so he knows
I'm all right. Poor Tommy, poor Tommy. I wish I
could help him—

I am opening the cupboard from which he took
the whisky bottle so many months ago, the one with
the two little red horses. I fill a glass halfway, put it
next to his chair on a table and touch his shoulder
again to reassure him . . . Then without looking
back I open the door and close it behind me.

He did not hit my face once. I am grateful for
that, because I would have hated it.

The girl at the desk sees me passing, wants to say
something but doesn't.

The rain has stopped so I can walk home. It
takes a long time because every step hurts. Not as if
I was sick. It's different. It hurts more, but I don't

feel sick at all. My lips are bleeding a bit, I must have bitten them so as not to cry out.

Why can't I cry? I should be screaming and sobbing and feeling desperate . . . It's not like that at all. I'll never never see him again, I won't even know what he does and whether he still thinks of me, I don't care, thank you God, for not letting me feel empty—I do not *care*. Loretta is gone and he is gone, gone, it is almost as if he'd never been, as if—I had woken up from one of my nightmares. It was necessary, like a thunderstorm is necessary to make the air pure and light again but no, I am not empty. In a strange way I know that life is only just beginning, that the real dream is yet to come . . . All the little devils and all the big monsters have gone and there is lots of lovely space for things to happen, oh yes so many things, so many "possibilities" . . .

It's good to walk alone in the dark. I can think better when I'm walking. Tommy in his armchair in the Clinic . . . that crumpled defeated figure. And me, me patting him on the back for comfort. Illo once gave mummie the latest book of a writer she adored and mummie loathed the book and said how *could* he. "Your precious darling has lost his halo," he told her with some satisfaction, "he's got feet of clay." I know what he meant. I think I've grown up. Tommy made me, even if he did not intend it this way.

When he was lying there, shaking and vulnerable, he became so different—small s m a l l . The wet blue shirt clinging to his back. That did something to me. It put me right off. The poor wretch, I thought, I've got to make it easier for him. That's why I went to fetch the whisky bottle. When he straightens up he will find it next to him and think: "I've beaten hell out of her and she is so kind." It was kind. That's the sort of thing a mother would do, not a child like me. A child? I just thought I had grown up. I did not feel like a child, making people do things they did not mean to. More like a puppet-master.

It's started raining again. I liked Tommy drying my hair, he took care of me then, just before . . . oh God! I don't want to think of it, I wish I were home. I want to be looked after. "Cut the cord," old Liebermann used to say to Loretta. Wonder what he meant. The cord to her father? To her mother more likely. She hardly ever mentioned her parents, except to say something nasty or sarcastic about them. She *is* odd. Of course, she would be odd, being a . . .

"Tags are for suitcases" is mummie's favourite quotation. All of a sudden I'm seeing luggage with labels circling round on the big turning table at London Airport, Illo smiling like a boy when he made a grab for our cases, mummie's and mine first. He's so unselfish, *he* wouldn't hurt a fly, let alone . . . My back, my back, it's burning like hell.

Will there be any marks, I wonder. I almost wish there were, just to remind me. As if I needed reminding.

The red lights dancing in his eyes, his arm lifting and swishing down again and again. I never cried. What did his face look like? What *is* his face like? His face, his face, I don't see it, I see bits and pieces, but I can't assemble it properly. It was always there the moment I woke up. Whatever I did, his face was hanging in front of me like a moon.

The rain has stopped, I feel cold. If only I was home. When mummie sees that I got wet she'll run a bath right away and bring me a hot coffee and a big towel, warm and soft. She'll put me to bed, maybe she'll read to me. I'd like a fairy tale, I always liked the Sleeping Princess best. Mummie would read on and on until I'm half asleep, her voice drifting away, her hands stroking my hair, I'm curling up under the blanket . . .

I open the front door and walk up the few steps to the flat. I don't need to hold on to the bannisters this time, I am quite strong.

Mummie is at home. I fling myself straight into her arms and start sobbing. She doesn't say anything, just strokes my hair and kisses me on the face . . . my mummie.

The door slams and she says: "There's Illo coming home." I can hear his key turning in the lock. Now he is standing by the door looking at us. He smiles seeing us both together like this, crying and

kissing, kissing and crying. I am so thirsty all of a
sudden, I could drink and drink forever. It's good
to be together when mummie is so nice and tender.
He might as well be nice to me too. I would not
like him kissing me, but I think it would be lovely
if he made me something to drink.

I feel very small in mummie's arms and so sleepy
and comfortable. But I don't want to sleep just yet.
I want to keep this new cosy feeling for a bit. I can
sleep all I want later. That's why I say very nicely
and very softly, half hidden in mummie's arms: "I
am so thirsty—I'd like something to drink, please.
Would you make us a great big jug of hot steaming
coffee with lots of sugar and milk—daddy?"